The Mills of God

WILLIAM H. ARMSTRONG

The Mills of God

Illustrated by David Armstrong

DOUBLEDAY & COMPANY, INC.
GARDEN CITY, NEW YORK, 1973

ISBN 0-385-00344-7 TRADE
0-385-04577-8 PREBOUND
LIBRARY OF CONGRESS CATALOG CARD NUMBER 72-95712

To Chris and Katie,
whose "Pa" illustrated this book.

Though the mills of God grind slowly,
  yet they grind exceeding small;
Though with patience He stands waiting,
  with exactness grinds He all.

                              F. von Logau
                    (LONGFELLOW'S TRANSLATION)

The Mills of God

Chapter One

When Aaron Skinner was twelve he spent most of the summer cutting cedar sprouts and digging thistles out of the hill pastures of Thomas Ruffner. The sheep which dotted Mr. Ruffner's hills as far as the eye could see, right to the foot of the mountain, kept the land clear except for cedars and thistles.

At the end of the summer, when Aaron Skinner had bought his own winter shoes, overalls, and the best winter jacket he had ever had, he still had fifteen dollars left. With this he bought a Blue Tick hound, a year old and trained for coons. The boy had had his heart set on a Black-and-Tan, like one in a calendar picture on the wall above his bed, but Matt Watts, the dog dealer, only had

Blue Ticks trained for coons. All his Black-and-Tans were trained for foxes.

The boy could not remember how long ago he had started dreaming of a dog to keep him company in the hills. It was, he thought, even before his brother Amos had died. For even with a brother two years younger to play with, the world of Aaron Skinner was a lonely world on a dead-end road called Dry Hollow, a world which was nothing more than a wrinkle in the vast fold of hills that belonged to Thomas Ruffner.

The hollow ended abruptly a few hundred yards past the boy's house. Two hills joined to form a V. From the point of the V a spring coursed its way along the clay-encrusted stones of a creek bed. In summer, about the time that the well at Aaron Skinner's house went dry and he had to carry water from the spring, the spring itself became little more than a trickle beyond the basin Aaron's father had shoveled out for the water pail and a drinking place for Mr. Ruffner's sheep.

The fact that for part of the winter and spring there was water enough to babble over the stones all the way to Buffalo Creek, a mile and a half away, did nothing to add life to the name Dry Hollow.

Around the bend of the road, perhaps a quarter mile below the Skinners' four-room, whitewashed, stilt-foundationed house, Ollie Cantrell lived with his peculiar mother. There was no other house until one came within sight of Buffalo Creek and the ribbon of road which followed the stream's course, dusty in summer and a series of overlapping and merging ruts in winter. Just at the end of the Dry Hollow Road, but within sight of the store, the several houses, and the blacksmith shop, all of which lined the banks of Buffalo Creek, stood the crumbling wreckage of what once had been the finest place thereabouts except the stark, square, jail-colored, stuccoed house of the region's biggest landowner, Thomas Ruffner.

This third house, near the fork where the Dry Hollow Road joined the Buffalo Creek Road, was known as the old Keck place. A modified replica of Mount Vernon, with overgrown boxwoods and ancient locust trees towering above the now-crumbling roof, it might have been easy to imagine the graceful living which enlivened the place in another day. But the story of the place conjured up a different picture. It was said to be haunted by the ghost of old Mrs. Keck, who had once ruled over a kingdom of slaves and cats. Her slaves she treated like animals, but her cats she treated like royal guests.

She had requested that, when she died, she be buried standing up on a hillside from which she could see her fields, the reason being that her slaves, knowing her ghost was watching, would not loaf at their work.

The crude cement tomb was still standing. The slaves had long since gone from the fields.

The house had never been lived in after the cat woman died. The land had passed through several owners. The house had now been almost a hundred years at its crumbling away. The property now belonged to Thomas Ruffner. He stored farm machinery under the sagging roof of the long veranda.

People said if one stood in front of the house at night and listened, the voice of the cat woman calling her cats

3

by name could be heard. Aaron Skinner tried to never pass the place after dark. Even if the sun was down and dusk gathering when he was late finding Ollie Cantrell's cow and bringing her home, he whistled as he passed, and always looked back several times until he got well beyond the house.

Once the boys in the village had told Aaron they would let him play baseball and go swimming with them in Buffalo Creek if he went through the Keck house alone. To be sure that he covered basement and attic, as well as the vast range of rooms with their casement windows and walnut paneling, they gave him a piece of chalk to put an A, for Aaron, on each door.

While he was inside they wired the front and back doors shut. When he finally escaped by crawling through a cellar window, they threw stones and chased him up the hollow, yelling, "Coward! Coward!" But the storekeeper told him later that they were too scared to ever go in and see if he had marked every door.

The boy's neighbor, Ollie Cantrell, was blind. He had been born that way and also deformed; he had a great hump on his back. Ollie Cantrell had spent his whole forty-five years in the hollow. He could find his way wherever he wanted to go, but Aaron Skinner liked to walk with him. He considered Ollie Cantrell, along with Mr. Hutton, the storekeeper, and Babe, the crippled boy who lived at the lower end of the village, his only true friends.

Aaron Skinner was like his father, Jake Skinner; he

4

was a very shy and quiet person. That's why the boys in the village went out of their way to pester him.

When he walked with Ollie they never threw rocks at him. Sometimes they would yell, "Ole humpback," at Ollie. Usually he would pretend he didn't hear them. But if he did say anything, it was something like, "Don't pay them no mind; they don't know no better." Once when Aaron started to tell Ollie who they were, he said, "Don't tell me. They ain't worth namin'. There's puppy dogs that has better names."

Aaron had heard his mother and father say, when they didn't know he was listening, that Ollie was born blind and deformed because his mother took laudanum. They had also said that Ollie didn't know who his father was and that his mother had never been married but had three dead babies buried in unmarked graves under the trees around her house. Aaron Skinner had looked for grave mounds. He had never seen anything that looked like one. What he heard only made him like Ollie more.

By Dry Hollow standards, Ollie Cantrell was prosperous even though he was blind. He made brooms and put new hickory seats in split-bottom chairs. He raised two hogs, bought two lambs from Mr. Ruffner and raised them to butcher, owned a cow, and had more than a dozen laying hens. There were also two rocking chairs on his porch, besides a porch swing. Jake Skinner's porch had a swing but no rocking chairs, only a straight-backed bench.

Sometimes Aaron sat and rocked with Ollie. Ollie's mother never came out of the house. Aaron brought

Ollie's cow home from grazing along the roadsides in exchange for a quart of milk each day. He had been doing it every day since he could remember, but he never had seen Ollie's mother outside.

There were things about going in search of Ollie Cantrell's brown Jersey cow every day which Aaron liked. It gave him a chance to escape the loneliness of the hollow in the summer months, when there was no school. And he always planned to start early so he would be on hand when the village boys, who loitered under the big sycamore tree across Buffalo Creek from the store, picked sides for baseball. If he was right there early, they would choose him and not throw rocks and drive him away or make him sit on the bank with Babe, the crippled boy, and get the ball when the catcher missed it and it went in the creek.

The boy also felt proud to carry home the molasses pail half filled with milk. He knew it was important to his mother in her struggle to "put food on the table" as she expressed her constant anxiety about "some day we're all goin' hungry." Once or twice Aaron had spilled it on the way home and she had been very angry and almost cried.

The things which disturbed and hurt Aaron Skinner about driving home Ollie Cantrell's cow, though, far outweighed the things he found agreeable. Only the very poor people, who lived in their whitewashed houses set on posts, with no land to pasture a cow, let their cows roam the roadsides, picking the sparse grass. People who had fields of their own resented the wandering cows reaching through their fences to get an added mouthful of grass. Aaron had heard talk at the store that there were getting to be so many cars on the road the State was just waiting for Hard Times to be over to pass a law forbidding cows to roam. Aaron would have been happy to lose the job of bringing home Ollie's cow, but he hoped Ollie would not have to get rid of his cow for lack of pasture. Aaron felt certain that he could help Ollie in other ways and still get milk to carry home. He wondered if Mr. Ruffner might rent Ollie Cantrell a couple acres for cow pasture, as Ollie had so often asked. Aaron didn't think he would, knowing Mr. Ruffner as he did. Mr. Ruffner let Jake Skinner fence in a lot to pasture his horse, but that was because he wanted Jake to have the horse for hauling wood from the land he cleared, making more and more hill pasture for Mr. Thomas Ruffner.

What he really thought important, day after day as he drove Ollie Cantrell's cow home, was not to ever let the boys in the village and the people at school know that it was somebody else's cow he drove. If they ever found that out, they would know he was poorer than just regular poor people, who grazed their cows in the road.

Sophie Skinner had often fussed at the boy's father about asking Mr. Ruffner if they could pasture a cow if they bought one. His father would always answer that they'd have to wait 'til Hard Times were over before they could buy one; then he'd speak to Mr. Ruffner.

Aaron Skinner had come to believe with his mother that "we was born to Hard Times, and we'll die with Hard Times." At the store the boy had heard men talking about a New Deal, with the government ending Hard Times. He didn't think the government knew about Dry Hollow or could find it if they wanted to. He wondered, too, what the difference would be between Hard Times and any other times. Hard Times were the only times he had ever known.

The Skinners raised only one hog, and although Sophie Skinner tried to raise some chickens every summer, she never got into fall with more than eight or ten hens, because of chicken hawks. Ollie Cantrell had trees around his place and they hid the hens from the soaring hawks. In Jake Skinner's worn dooryard nothing grew to provide cover.

Besides two split-bottom rockers, which stayed on the porch all the time, even in winter, Aaron Skinner measured Ollie Cantrell's prosperity in other ways. When Ollie walked out to the store for broom wire or to take new brooms to be sold, he always asked the boy to go along. Aaron knew it was just for company, for the blind man knew every stone, every fence, every gate through Ruffner's short cut along the way, and never missed the turn which went over the bridge to the store.

Inside the store Ollie would feel the flat-topped cooler which stood alongside the counter, tap it with his walking stick, and say, "Have a Coke to drink, Aaron?" And then, just when the boy had made his Coke last as long as he could and Ollie heard the empty bottle hit in the wooden case under the cooler, he would buy ten cents' worth of chocolate drops or stick candy, alternating each trip and never forgetting. He would give the poke to

8

the boy, not taking any for himself, saying as he did, "Save half for your sister Sara and little brother Seth."

Aaron always got home with even more than half. For when he rattled the poke taking out a piece on the way home, Ollie would never take a piece when the boy offered it. So after one or two pieces Aaron would close the poke and not eat any more himself. At home he'd count out equal shares to Sara and Seth, with a little extra for Sara if she'd carried in his stove wood. He'd offer his mother some, and his father, too, if it was after sundown and he was home from work. His mother would say, "No, it'll hurt my bad teeth." His father would say, "No, son, you keep it."

But the luxury of the Coca-Cola from the flat-topped cooler with the opener on the side, where the bottle fizzed when opened, was the thing that showed Ollie's prosperity more than anything else. For Aaron would sit on the lid of the horseshoe and hardware bins and drink and study the fizz. He turned the bottle in his hand and felt as rich as anybody until it was empty and the fizz all gone. Then he could stand and stare at the candy and chewing gum, because Ollie couldn't see him and think he was hinting.

When he went to the store with his father, he never got a Coke. Sometimes his father would buy a nickel's worth of gum drops. You got more gum drops for your money than chocolate or stick candy. When Aaron went to the store with his father, he almost never stood in front of the candy and chewing gum case looking through the dirty glass. He didn't want his father to be hurt if he didn't have a spare nickel.

9

By the time Aaron was eight or nine he understood a lot about Jake and Sophie Skinner's feelings. He took in everything they talked about, even when they didn't know he was listening. Sometimes the talk he wasn't supposed to hear made him feel older than he was.

Chapter Two

The store on the banks of Buffalo Creek was the center of social and economic life for the village and the people who lived in the hills and up and down the creek. Here eggs and butter, culled laying hens, and surplus grain were traded for everything from thread to halter rope, from vanilla extract to liver pills, from horseshoes to cookstoves. Here the people like Jake Skinner came on Saturday night with their weekly pay, paid for the flour, sugar, coffee, and side meat from the week past, and usually had nothing left over. Sometimes when they paid their bill the storekeeper would pass them a two-cent Virginia Dare cigar.

Whether Aaron was with Ollie, with his father, or alone, the store and the storekeeper, Mr. Hutton, provided color and interest for the generally colorless and barren life of Aaron Skinner. The storekeeper was always willing to tell Aaron which way Ollie's cow went when she came out of the hollow.

He had heard talk at the store that President Roosevelt was going to make electricity available in the country. Aaron wondered how the store would look lighted as bright as day. Part of its fascination was the dim light that came from two dirty and fly-specked windows at the front and back, leaving the middle of the eighty-foot-long building in light so dim that many a customer carried goods to the front or the back of the store to examine them. The building had been extended as demand for space grew. Since there was a steep bank on one side and Buffalo Creek on the other, it was always extended lengthwise. This accounted for the great length.

The muted yellow light which came from the four great, tin-shaded oil lamps, suspended from their iron hooks in the beaded-pine ceiling, made the store brighter at night than in daylight. The lamplight also provided an assortment of shadows of dry-goods shelves, broom racks, stovepipe, milk pails, horse collars, and automobile tires hanging together. These ghostly-still shadows were absent during the day.

Near the center of the long building a mottled rust-

and-tobacco-juice-colored stove stood on a slab of cement. In winter it was surrounded by nail kegs, where men with corncob pipes puffed away, watching the heat waves of the giant stove carry their smoke clouds up to the ceiling. In summer they moved to the end of the store porch farthest from the hand-cranked gas pump— this at the request of the storekeeper.

Sometimes Ollie Cantrell would sit briefly with the loafers. Aaron had also known his father to sit for a while on a Saturday night when he had paid his bill and the storekeeper would pass the box of two-cent cigars over the counter and say, "Here, Jake, have a cigar."

The boy was so very proud when he saw his father join the circle and light up his cigar. Aaron never went closer to the circle than listening-distance. As much as his shyness, he had the feeling that this was a right that came with manhood.

His day would come. One day he would walk out of the hollow with his extra shirt and socks in a paper bag. He would get a ride over the mountain in the bakery truck. After he had worked a few weeks at the paper mill, he could come back wearing a whole suit with a vest and paying for what he bought with greenbacks from a pocketbook for folding money. Then he would join the circle with a whole quarter's worth of cheese and crackers.

Then other mouths would water as his had so often. Somebody in the circle would say, "Well, Aaron, I guess you're makin' it pretty good." And he'd answer, "Yep. Forty cents an hour for an eight-hour day, five days a week. A dollar a day for room and board. Pay envelope every two weeks." The boy had listened to Isaac Eastman and the Horton boys tell their success stories. Ike Eastman had been at the paper mill since he was big enough to lie about his age. People in the village said he'd had money buried somewhere when he died. Said he had a lot more than he lost when the bank went broke.

But, for now, the spot where Aaron stood near the front counter held its own interests. Here the spool of tying cord whirled on the peg which held it when the storekeeper tied up a pound of coffee or five pounds of sugar. The coffee grinder, with a few spots still showing its once bright-red paint, had a balance wheel which kept turning, with its curved spokes making their moving pattern, long after the storekeeper had stopped turning the crank and taken the paper poke of freshly ground coffee beans from under the spout.

Here, too, the smells were more pungent. Besides the aroma of newly ground coffee, there was the great round of cheese, as yellow as a ripe wheatfield, with its missing V where some had been cut out, and the broad, blunt-ended knife stuck in the top. Nearby was the mackerel keg with its thick brine sending up the smell of the sea, made even more pungent for the boy as he studied the sailing ship etched in charcoal on the side of the key.

The machine for cutting chewing tobacco stood next to the coffee grinder. Its action always made the boy flinch, for he knew the razor-sharp blade, moving in its iron frame like a guillotine but powered by a lever rather than weight, would take off a finger, bone and all, in the bat of an eye.

About the middle of each tobacco plug there was a

14

tiny metal symbol of its trademark. The storekeeper sold Red Mule and Lucky Jim. If a chewer bought a half plug of Red Mule, the little red mule would usually lose its head or tail in the plug cutter. Lucky Jim was a fisherman perched on a rock. A half plug of Lucky Jim would sometimes cost Jim his head or his seat.

The plug cutter was also used to cut strap leather if somebody wanted to make a bell strap or a dog collar without buying one ready made. But whatever it was, the cutting prompted Aaron to put his hands deep in his pockets.

The color and excitement the store provided for Aaron Skinner was surpassed only by a ride to town with Mr. Hutton. When the storekeeper was going to town to get supplies at the wholesale house and take butter and eggs that he'd taken in for store goods, he'd stop where Babe, the crippled boy, and Aaron sat on the bank watching the village boys playing baseball or pitching horseshoes, and ask Aaron if he wanted to ride to town.

Mr. Hutton never asked Babe to go. Aaron felt sorry sometimes that he didn't. He thought it was because Babe stammered when he talked and was very hard to understand.

Aaron could understand him, for they spent a lot of time sitting together when the other boys wouldn't let them play. They didn't have much to talk about except the same things over and over again. So Aaron got to understand Babe as well as anybody. Except when the boys threw rocks at him, or called him names, or mocked the way he talked or walked, dragging the foot that was turned sideways; then his stammer was nothing but a hissing and sputtering that not even Aaron could understand.

Babe didn't have a very good memory, and this made it easy for the village boys to do the same cruel tricks over and over. Two of them would bend over and one would call out real loud, "Look what I found" or "This is the funniest-lookin' bug I ever saw." Babe would walk over and look. Then a third boy would get down on his hands and knees behind him. The two would rise up suddenly and push Babe backward over the kneeling boy. He would hit the ground head first on his back awfully hard. Sometimes blood would come out of his mouth as he limped away sputtering and crying. That's how he got the nickname Babe. He was two or three years older than Aaron, who never cried when he was hurt. But to make Babe cry was a great victory for the boys.

Aaron had thought he might say to Mr. Hutton, the storekeeper, "Wouldn't you like to let Babe go too?" There was plenty of room for three in the pickup-truck cab. But Aaron's mother had said, "You tend to your own business and don't meddle."

Aaron was afraid, too, that if he said that, Mr. Hutton might think he didn't care whether he got to go or not. And except for the church picnic, which Aaron had been to only twice, this trip to town was about as exciting as anything he knew.

The smells at the wholesale house, the big ice-cream machine at the creamery, where Mr. Hutton took the butter, the cases filled with pocket knives and guns at the hardware store, where he picked up kegs of nails, hog rings, stovepipe, and cooking ware — Aaron could never decide which he liked best.

At the creamery Mr. Hutton would put his hand on the boy's shoulder and push him into the doorway of the chocolate-smelling room where unfrozen ice cream poured out of a big spout into five- and ten-gallon cans. "You're too timid for your own good, boy," Mr. Hutton would say. "Get right in there where the free ice cream is."

The push on the shoulder made the boy feel warm and soft all over. The shy fear that made him cold disappeared, the knotty feeling that he often felt in his mind and in his throat smoothed out into a softness that he did not feel very often.

Three men worked at the creamery. If the right one was there, he'd reach up and take a dipper off the hook and hand it to the boy, saying as he did, "There you are. Now fill up while she's pourin'." If either of the other two men were running the machine, they wouldn't pay any attention until Mr. Hutton would say, "You got a boy here who wants to sample that flavor." Then they would take the dipper and hardly get more than enough to cover the bottom of the dipper and pass it to the boy. "Put it in the sink there when you finish," was all they ever said. Aaron always hoped the pleasant man who smiled and said, "Now fill up while she's pourin'" would be running the machine.

When Aaron had finished with the dipper he always remembered to thank the man. But he spoke very softly. Sometimes when they were alone again Mr. Hutton would say, "You have to learn to speak out, son. You're too timid. If you'd speak out and fight back, the boys wouldn't pester you the way they do Babe." Aaron wished he could speak out like Mr. Hutton. Even the way he sometimes said to Aaron's father, "No, Jake, I can't let you have any more credit until you pay up." "It was what he had to do," the boy always told himself.

The hardware store was a dreamland. There Aaron looked and looked. Besides the knives and guns and fishing poles, there was a big picture calendar with a hunter sitting on a log at the edge of a vast forest. Two beautiful Black-and-Tan hounds stood nearby with their ears cocked and their noses stretched to the air. Underneath was written *The Scent at Dawn.* Far away, beyond the forest and over the distant hills, it showed the sun just coloring the sky a beautiful pink.

After Aaron had been looking at the picture for so many of his trips with Mr. Hutton, one of the clerks in the store said, "You really like that picture. When the year's over and we get a new calendar, I'll send it to you by Mr. Hutton, or keep it 'til you come. You don't come much in winter because of school. I'll send it."

It was just one week after New Year's when Mr. Hutton called across to where the school bus stopped and said, "I've got your picture."

The creamery and the hardware store afforded their particular tastes and dreams, but Aaron's third stop with Mr. Hutton, the storekeeper, was a visit to the storehouse of the world, like Pharaoh's granaries, which Aaron had studied about in his schoolbooks.

The third stop was always the wholesale house. Here the mouth-watering smell of brown sugar in hundred-pound sacks and shelves of baker's chocolate and Hershey bars mixed to make what Aaron was sure heaven must smell like. Boxes containing hundreds of plugs of Red Mule and Lucky Jim chewing tobacco gave off a bittersweet, mellow aroma. Great stacks of rounds of cheese sent a sharp, rancid air from one end of the building to the other. There were also sacks of coffee beans and the musty smell of paper bags, twine, hemp rope, and cloth. But nothing could taint the smell of brown sugar and chocolate. And long after Mr. Hutton had loaded his provisions and the man and boy were on the road, Aaron kept the memory and tasted it.

There were other things at the wholesale house which stirred Aaron's imagination besides the awareness that there was candy enough to keep a boy supplied forever, and enough beans, sugar, and flour that if a person had them he would never be hungry or have to ask for credit at the store. In every corner and by every row of sacks there were rattraps, always set and baited with cheese, but Aaron had never seen a rat in any of them. There were so many cats that Aaron had given up trying to count them. They were curled up on bean sacks, stretched on windowsills, and pacing the narrow corridors between miles and miles of cardboard boxes. How the cats avoided the traps was a mystery which continued to puzzle him even after the man at the wholesale house said that cats didn't like cheese.

The visit to the wholesale house reached its climax when Mr. Hutton and the boy went to the office to pay for the goods. The man at the stand-up desk would take a small wooden pail from the desk top and pass it to

Aaron. It was always full of Tootsie Rolls or Hershey's Chocolate Kisses. The boy would take one. At that, the man would tilt the pail so that both Aaron's hands were needed to keep the candy from pouring on the floor. "That's right, take a handful," the man would say. And by that time the boy's two hands were spilling over.

The creamery was nice when the right man was operating the ice-cream machine. But nothing could equal the visit to the wholesale house.

The last stop Mr. Hutton made was the ice plant. It was just across the railroad tracks, at the edge of town. Here he bought a hundred-pound block of ice to put in the flat-topped soda-pop cooler at the store. The man at the ice plant would open a thick door and stick an iron hook into a huge block of ice. Splinters and small chunks would fly off as he dragged it to the doorway. He would kick one of the chunks toward Aaron and say, "Cool off." If it was too big for his mouth, Aaron would hold it in one hand and then the other, sucking all the while to get it down to mouth size. It was more fun when he could hold it in his mouth, roll it from side to side, and cool his throat all the way down with Tootsie Roll- or Hershey Kiss-flavored ice water.

Each year just after school started, it was county fair time. There was one day off from school for school children to get in for half price. Aaron had never gone, but almost everybody did. When they came back and talked about cotton candy and molasses-popcorn balls, he envied them a little, but not much. None of them had ever had a trip to town with the storekeeper in his pickup truck.

Chapter Three

"This dog is trained for silent trailin'," Matt Watts
boasted to the boy. "He's hunted with ole Split-ear, and
ole Split-ear has surprised a lot of coons. And if this dog
don't work out, you can bring him back and get your
money. Why, you oughta get thirty or forty coons this
season."

"I'd hoped to be able to get a dog and a secondhand .22 rifle for my money. You ain't got another dog and a gun for that much, have you?" the boy asked. He doubted that as many coons could be cornered on the ground as Matt said. He needed a rifle to shoot the ones his dog would drive up a tree.

Aaron's dream of owning a gun was not as strong or as old as his dream for a dog. With a gun he might be able to get at least thirty raccoon hides to sell. That would be about sixty dollars. With sixty dollars he would be ready when spring came. He could buy new khaki pants and a blue cambric shirt, and shed his winter clothes when the other boys at school did. Then they wouldn't laugh at him. He might even be able to buy a pair of Red Ball tennis shoes.

The line that separated those who wore Red Ball tennis shoes after spring mud dried up and those who went barefoot was generally the line that separated the "very poor" from the "not that poor." There were some exceptions, like the doctor's boy, who could have afforded tennis shoes, even with crepe soles, but chose to go barefoot.

Aaron knew he would accept his barefoot status even if he had enough hide-money left over to buy summer shoes. He would give it to his mother to help buy gingham for sister Sara, who was three years behind him, for a dress, and pants and shirt for his little brother Seth, who was two years behind Sara.

"You can't git no dog and gun for only fifteen dollars," Matt Watts said with an air of growing impatience as he looped a noose of binder twine over the young dog's head and dragged him from a hogpen that substituted for a kennel.

When the boy saw the dog in the full light of day, he felt his money, still folded in his pocket, and thought of changing his mind. Every rib showed under the blue-tick skin, which did not show its blue dots on a white hide, but rather a mangy, mud-and-dirt-encrusted gray. The dog sank to his belly with his tail between his legs. He gagged as Matt Watts jerked him forward by the tightening noose.

The boy felt the new collar neatly rolled up in his pocket. He had bought it and a chain a year before he had money to buy the dog. He knelt and rubbed his hand over the dog's head. The cowed creature raised his nose, licked the boy's hand, and pushed one front paw forward as though he might get to his feet. Now the boy knew that he would buy the dog; if for no other reason, just to get him out of the cruel hands of Matt Watts.

"What's his name?" the boy asked as he took the rope from Matt Watts and continued to pet the dog.

"I just call him Tick, but I ain't called him much except when he's hunted with ole Split-ear. I doubt if he knows his name. I want the cash if you're gonna buy. I said that before, didn't I?"

Aaron got to his feet, and the dog did too. The dog took a step toward the boy and wagged his tail. The boy started to take his new collar from his pocket but did not. Looking at the dog's skinny neck he had decided the collar would hang so loosely that Matt Watts would laugh.

"The money is all there," the boy said as he handed

the man a roll of bills tied with a piece of string. "And you say I can bring him back if he don't hunt right?" the boy asked halfheartedly, all the while thinking that he would never part with his new dog.

"That's my guarantee, as I said before. If he don't work out, you can bring him back. Why, you oughta get even more coons than I speculate."

The dog grew bolder by the minute. He moved his front paws forward and stretched himself after the manner of a well-fed hound just awakened from sleeping in the sun by a kitchen door, smelling ham frying on the stove and dreaming of the chase.

Matt Watts carefully leafed through the fifteen one-dollar bills. The boy was adding up more money too.

He'd still have money left if he sold as many as thirty coon hides. Why, a gun and his spring clothes and what he'd give his mother for Sara and Seth would still leave enough to buy a baseball glove of his own. No, he'd buy a catcher's mitt. That's what the boys in the village didn't have. Then they'd let him play and he wouldn't just have to get the ball when it went in the creek. And if he could get a bat and ball too, they'd be yellin' to him when he came down the Dry Hollow Road, "Hurry up, Aaron, we've been waiting for you."

"I don't think Tick is a very good name," the boy said now that he was owner and was feeling the impulse of owner's confidence. "I'm going to call him Rowdy. Come on, Rowdy, we're going home."

"He'll come when he's hungry whatever you call him," Matt Watts said as he slapped his sides and guffawed at his own joke.

Aaron did not have to lead Rowdy. Instead he had to hold him back. Rowdy seemed anxious to leave Matt Watts.

"Don't worry, Rowdy, good puppy," the boy said as he quickened his pace, "you'll never see this place again."

When the boy was out of sight of Matt Watts's place he took the binder-twine noose from around Rowdy's neck. He buckled on the new brass-studded collar he had kept in his pocket while he was at Matt's. Rowdy was so skinny that, even buckled in the last hole, it hung so loosely on his neck that Aaron knew it would be lost by falling off over his head. He would have to take it back to the store and exchange it for a smaller one.

Aaron counted the ribs and the saw-tooth ridges along Rowdy's spine. The way home had to keep Rowdy out of sight of the curious and the cruel. Aaron would leave the Buffalo Creek Road about a half mile before he came to the store. If he met anybody on the five-and-a-half-mile walk from Matt Watts's place to where they would turn and cross Thomas Ruffner's fields to hit his Dry Hollow Road, he would slip into the bushes or hide behind fences. His skeletonlike dog would not be made fun of; he would avoid the store above everything else.

There would be people sitting in the September sun on the end of the store porch away from the gas pump. They would laugh at Rowdy and make remarks about him to taunt Aaron: "Better give that hound a bath there, Skinner, he smells like a pigpen" or "Better take a tire pump and pump that hound up some, he's sorta flat." "Why, if that dog ever smelled a scent and give chase, he'd run right outa that collar, he's so skinny." Aaron would not go home by the store.

Aaron left the Buffalo Creek Road. He went down the bank to the edge of the Creek. There he let Rowdy drink, then led him into the water. With his hands he dipped up water and poured it over Rowdy. He scrubbed the mangy, dirt-encrusted hide with his hands. Rowdy seemed to enjoy it. He wagged his tail and jumped around until Aaron was almost as wet as his dog. Rowdy looked a lot better when he had been washed. But the ribs still showed. He was still a rack of bones. People in the village would laugh at him.

The boy and the dog sat on the bank, drying in the sun. The blue-tick dots showed up quite distinctly on the white background. "You're a true Blue Tick, Rowdy," the boy said as he rubbed his hand along the backbone, showing its spiny ridge. "And nobody better not laugh at you." The boy pondered how to get Rowdy past the village and home unnoticed. Then, in a week or two, he'd be fattened up and the boy would take him everywhere and be proud to show him off.

Ollie Cantrell had been excited about the dog when Aaron told him he was going to buy it. He would persuade Ollie to let him leave Rowdy at his house for a week or two. He would trade Ollie work for milk to help fatten Rowdy up before he took him home. If he took him home the way he was now, his mother would say he hadn't got much for his money. The boy had seen Ollie giving his hogs milk, so he knew there was more than Ollie and his mother used. He would slip some of his own biscuits into his pocket at each meal and bring them to Rowdy.

Matt Watts had said, "Feed him on corn meal mixed with water. That's all he's ever had."

"You're dry," the boy said to the dog as he ran his hand over his head and along his back. "And you'll never have to eat corn meal and water again. Ollie can't see how poor you are, and we'll cut through the fields and miss the village. I'll tie you with a rope at Ollie's and get you a collar that fits some other time. We won't go home by the village today. Come on, boy. We'll keep to the road until we're almost at the store, then we'll cross Mr. Ruffner's lower fields and come out on the Dry Hollow Road. That way nobody will see us and meddle in our business."

The dog jumped in circles around the boy. "I named you right," the boy said. "You are rowdy."

Before Aaron came in sight of the village he climbed the fence into one of Thomas Ruffner's fields. By crossing two or three fields he could come out almost halfway home on the Dry Hollow Road.

Chapter Four

The dog caused the boy to almost trip and fall several times. After the washing and rubbing in the sun it seemed that Rowdy couldn't walk close enough to his new master. The new collar hung loosely on the dog's neck and the chain dangled freely in the boy's hand. After Aaron had become entangled several times by Rowdy circling and looking up into his eyes, the boy unbuckled the collar, wiped both sides of it on his pants, then rolled it up and put it in his pocket.

"You wouldn't run away, would you, Rowdy? I have to keep this collar new-lookin' so I can trade it for one that fits. Old Matt Watts said you'd have to be chained for several weeks or you'd run back home. Maybe where you're goin' ain't much, but it's better'n what you had." Rowdy's head was tilted to one side, his ears cocked for listening. The boy smiled down at him and gave a subdued sigh of pleasure. The dog wagged his tail and dropped his ears; he understood.

The crest of the field where the boy had stopped gave him a view of Thomas Ruffner's house and the long barns with their red roofs. In the other direction lay the village. Both were far enough away that the boy felt no fear of being seen or any urgency to hurry. The feeling of loneliness that drove him to try day after day to join the boys in the village was for the moment gone. He was content to sit under the tall locust tree which crowned the crest of the field and enjoy a new-found peace.

In the distance a thin line of dark smoke rose a little higher than the church spire, then wavered and folded back upon itself to form a smudge on the faraway blue of the late-summer sky. "Coal smoke from Carter's bellows," the boy said to himself.

At the village store the boy had listened to a lot of talk about how times were changing the day a gas pump had been put in front of Carter's blacksmith shop and a big sign at the edge of the roof, with the picture of an Overland touring car with its top down, announced Carter's Garage. But Jake Skinner still had his work horse, Ole

Charlie, shod there and his one-horse wagon steel-tired about every second year.

If one had been asked to define the limits of the village, it perhaps would have been the store at one end and the blacksmith shop at the other. In the half mile between these there were strung along both sides of the creek a dozen houses, the church, a deserted mill which housed the post office in one corner, and an abandoned two-room school building the Mormons had bought and used for a meetinghouse.

Some, however, said the village was four miles long and roadside wide. The main road followed Buffalo Creek at right angles from the Dry Hollow Road. It stretched for four miles before it turned over the hills toward the town. Houses were scattered along the whole length of the road at intervals long ago determined by the amount of land required to provide a living for the householder. This pattern had long since been broken by bad luck, bad management, and a thousand ifs and excuses. Now there was almost no land left with some of the houses. The people who lived in these worked for people like Thomas Ruffner — people who always seemed to get ahead.

At the end of the four-mile wandering of the Buffalo Creek Road by the side of the stream, and just before it left the narrow valley and turned over the hills toward the town, there was a village not unlike Aaron Skinner's. It was called South Buffalo, and the two main differences were that the mill in South Buffalo was still in operation, and there was no blacksmith shop. The church there was smaller than at North Buffalo and of a different denomination. The two-room schoolhouse had been taken over for a voting place and a justice-of-the-peace court. Aaron had heard men talking at the store about how a place for holding court was bad. Before that, neighbors settled their differences peacefully. But after they got a place for the justice of the peace to settle cases, somebody was swearing out a warrant for his neighbor every week.

From where Aaron Skinner sat under the locust tree at the crest of one of Thomas Ruffner's rolling pastures he could pick out the roof of the consolidated schoolhouse almost two miles away, set midway between Aaron's village and South Buffalo, so as to serve both. It was about a mile and a half below the end of the Dry Hollow Road, so Aaron and his little sister and brother rode the bus after they had walked out of the hollow. Sometimes they missed the bus. When they did, Aaron would send Sara and Seth back home, but he always went on.

He liked school even though the boys from the village picked on him at recess if the teachers weren't watching. School was a way of escaping the loneliness which was forever pouring down with the shadows of the hills, filling the hollow. And over against the terror of being called on to read or spell before the class, which choked him with fear, there was the strange fascination of the house across the creek from the school, where the sad tunes of a player piano had replaced the merry ones after the death from typhoid fever of the little girl who lived there. When Aaron caught the faint sound of the distant music, he would slip away to the corner of the school lot, hide behind a tree so as not to be disturbed, and listen until the bell sounded to end recess. The player piano was the only music he had ever heard besides the organ in the church, which wheezed and sighed when a lady pumped it. When the Sanford girl had died, Aaron's teacher had talked about it in class and said she was in heaven, where there was no night and no day, where there was no sickness, hunger, or want, and where there was angelic music carried on a breeze which never brought storm or chill. Aaron thought the music which came from the house was just like the angelic music his teacher had described.

The Sanford house itself was just right for the heavenly music, the boy thought. All the houses along the creek were either L-shaped farmhouses painted white with green shutters or tiny, rectangular-shaped tenant houses with their shed-roofed kitchen extensions, whitewashed or left to weather their brownish gray; all except the house of Thomas Ruffner, the crumbling Keck house, and the Sanford house. Thomas Ruffner's house was square and big, stuccoed, with chimneys on either side which looked too big even against the broad side of the house, with its equally ill-proportioned small windows left shutterless.

But the Sanford house was different. It had dormer windows which came out of the roof. The windowlights were diamond-shaped, and the downstairs windows were very wide, three windows in a row. The roof extended far out over the house, and there were fancy brackets between the house and roof. On the porch there were large, round porch posts in pairs, and there was glass on each side and above the front door. The house was painted dark gray with bright-yellow shutters. Not even in the town, where Aaron went with the storekeeper, when he went in his truck to get goods to sell, had Aaron ever found such a beautiful house. Since Cissie Sanford died, he had never seen anyone playing on the wide lawn, which went all the way down to the creek and had a stone wall with steps right to the edge of the water.

Once Cissie Sanford had smiled at him in line at recess. After that he had looked at her a lot without letting her know that he was looking. For two years he had thought each summer that when school started he would pick a desk right behind or just across the aisle from her. In summer he used to hope he'd find Ollie's cow down this way. This was always the first way he looked. He hoped the cow would be above Cissie Sanford's house, so she wouldn't see him driving the cow home. In summer he had stood behind the willow trees between the road and the creek and listened to the happy music that came from the player piano. Now the music that came out was sad, like a funeral with the lady pumping the church organ, without the wheezing. But the music reminded Aaron that heaven must be a wonderful place to be if it was like the teacher said. He'd heard his mother talk of God's lightnin' strikin', but he was sure that was on earth and wouldn't be in heaven. When his mother said, "A body would be better off dead," she was probably talkin' about heaven.

The boy and his dog moved with a subdued, dreamlike pace across the second field, the boy lost in his daydreams too much to please Rowdy, who wanted to romp. From the edge of the second field the dry creek bed with its sycamores could be seen in the distance, across one more pasture. Along the creek bed there was a short cut through other fields to Aaron Skinner's house. The boy interrupted his thoughts long enough to take in where he was and say to the dog, "Not much longer now, Rowdy, boy, and I'll be fixin' you a pallet in Ollie Cantrell's cowshed. Then, when you look a little more worth the price, so Ma won't make me take you back, you'll have a home and a pallet right under my bed. Or if Ma objects, in a box by the door on the porch."

The road which ended at Jake Skinner's house went past Ollie Cantrell's, then climbed to the crest of the eastern ridge and followed the ridge until it descended to the Buffalo Creek Valley. All the land on the eastern side of the road had once belonged to the Keck place; that on the west side had been inherited by Thomas Ruffner from his father. Now Thomas Ruffner owned all the land.

The ascent and descent of the road, dividing the two properties, made it two miles long. But Thomas Ruffner had allowed Jake Skinner to put gates through the several fields in the hollow along the creek bed, making the path a half mile shorter than the road and level for walking.

"Keep the gates closed and there'll be no trouble," Aaron's father was always cautioning him. "And don't go in any cattle pastures, 'cause he lets his bulls run free and they're mean. There's only sheep in the fields where the short cut goes through."

Aaron Skinner had inherited his timid nature from his father. Jake Skinner was a soft-spoken, mild, and quiet man. Even at the age of twelve Aaron Skinner, studying his father's face when he rested on the porch or by the kitchen stove after his long day in the fields for Thomas Ruffner, knew there was no spark of dream left to lighten the drawn, weathered face. Whatever bitterness needed voice was left for Sophie Skinner.

The boy wished his father was not afraid of Thomas Ruffner. Sometimes when Mr. Ruffner spoke harshly to his father, and his father only answered, "Yes," the boy wanted to speak up, but he never did.

Thomas Ruffner was a stern, demanding man with cold eyes and a mouth that drooped with a stonelike permanence. He rode a taller than average horse, a raw-boned roan stallion with a twitchy mouth and earth-pawing front feet, never still.

Aaron had asked Ollie Cantrell, since he never talked to his father about Tom Ruffner, why Thomas Ruffner used a stallion for a riding horse; no one else did. Ollie had said maybe it gave him a feeling of power and strength. Aaron thought Ollie was right. Thomas Ruffner was always striking the horse on the side of the head with a stout switch he carried to make the stallion stop rattling the bit between its teeth. The eye on the side he struck was blind from being hit so often. The eyeball and the white around it had run together into a milky mass.

And just like Mr. Ruffner's blue Hupmobile was the biggest car up and down the creek, his saddle was something special — a Kentucky-field with hooded stirrups, the quality of the leather spoken for by the sound of fine tanning as stirrup strap rubbed against girth buckle when Ruffner rose in the stirrups to look down on Jake

Skinner toiling in Ruffner's fields. When he said, "Will you finish here today?" always just as he was about to gallop away before the man could answer, it sounded to Aaron Skinner the same as if he had ordered, "Get finished here today!" The boy wondered if it sounded that way to his father. He hated Thomas Ruffner for riding away before his father could answer. He wished Mr. Ruffner would stay long enough for his father to throw down whatever tool he was using and say, "If you want it finished today, finish it yourself." But when Aaron Skinner finished his wishful dreaming, he was glad Mr. Ruffner rode away quickly. It saved him added minutes of hurting for Jake Skinner.

The boy and his dog were now at the crest of the slope which went down to the dry creek bed with its line of sycamores. Since they were crossing fields, not a part of the short cut allowed, the boy had kept a sharp lookout for the tall roan stallion and its rider. Now he studied the landscape for any movement around the distant gray house and the clustered barns with their red roofs glistening in the September sun. Nothing moved. Thomas Ruffner's sleek cattle and fleecy sheep, which usually dotted and punctuated the land, had found shade.

Once the boy started down the slope he would not be able to see a rider approach from the direction of the house. Seeing the barns reminded the boy of something that happened each spring. Something that he told himself he would never do again, but always did.

When young ewes lambed in the field, they often deserted their lambs at eveningtime to follow the flock to the feeding trough in the sheep barn. Aaron Skinner, hearing the panicky and childlike cry of a lost lamb riding the spring breeze over the land, would find the scared one huddled in some fence corner. Then, far across the fields to Tom Ruffner's big, stuccoed house the boy would carry his prize, folded in his arms, stroking the soft white fleece, trying to quiet the frightened baby. The boy would talk to the lamb as he walked. "Don't cry, little one, you'll soon be back with your mother."

Aaron had carried the first lambs home to their mothers when he was five or six. And each year he did it, for the next four or five years, his dream of what Mr. Ruffner would one time do remained alive.

Mr. Ruffner would suddenly realize how many lambs had been saved. He would come from the big house, smile at Aaron and say, "You're a good shepherd, Aaron!" He'd call him by his name instead of "boy." "When that lamb is old enough to be weaned it's going to be yours. I'll put an S for Skinner on its rump in marker paint rather than R for Ruffner. And since one lamb frets of loneliness and doesn't do very well, I'll give you another. After all, how many have you saved for me? Besides, it takes two lambs to jump and race and play leapfrog."

But one lambing season came and went, and then another, but Aaron never heard his dream words from Thomas Ruffner. All he ever heard was, "Ah! the damn dumb sheep." And sometimes Mr. Ruffner shook his finger close up in Aaron's face and said, "Are you sure you didn't carry that lamb home for a pet and Jake made you bring it back when he came from work? Don't you ever do that, boy."

By the time Aaron Skinner was ten or eleven he gave

up his dream of ever carrying home a lamb and an-
nouncing, "It's mine," and saying to Sara and Seth, "you
can pet it all you want. But don't squeeze it!"

Now the boy tried not to even pretend that he heard
the distressed and lonely cry. It would be blind Ollie
Cantrell, as the two stood together at Ollie's cowshed
gate after milking, who would say, "Hear that faint cry?"
And the boy would hesitate and question if there really
was a cry. Then he would say, "I have to take the milk
home first."

When the boy was younger, he used to marvel at his
blind friend Ollie. He always faced the west when they
stood by the cowshed door after milking. And he would
ask the boy, "Is the sunset pink or red or gold, and what
color does it make the hills?"

But Aaron Skinner's answers slowly lost their warmth
and color until Ollie no longer asked. The blind man saw
a slow poisoning turn sweetness to bitterness in the heart
of the boy. He dreaded the worst. For blind Ollie Cantrell knew that unless a part of the child was kept alive
in the heart, it would encrust itself with gall and turn to
stone. Then there's only the death of a day, and no longer
is there a glorious birth of twilight.

Ollie would call after the boy as he started home with
his milk pail, "It'll get awfully chilly up there tonight. If
that lamb doesn't get its mother's milk to keep it warm,
it'll be dead by morning."

Thoughts of a lamb dead, stiff and cold to the touch,
like Aaron's brother when he died with whooping cough
in bed with Aaron, would send the boy again into the hill
pasture. The boy noticed that the cry always grew more

plaintive and scared as the shadows grew darker in the hills.

And the behavior of the lost lamb changed too. When the boy came in the daylight, the lamb would run to him and smell about his feet as if to smell out some new source of milk. But coming in the twilight, the boy became some dreaded enemy. The tiny white ball of wool would try to run away, dodging this way and that, trying to escape some predator left over from nature's training for survival before there were good shepherds.

The boy no longer knocked on Thomas Ruffner's kitchen door and had his words formed and ready when the door opened with a jerk amid the sound of boot heels hard upon the floor, "I've brought a lost lamb home, Mr. Ruffner." Instead he slipped stealthfully, like a thief, through the sheep-lot gate to the open door of the sheep barn. There, with furtive glances toward the house, he would crouch in mingled fear and wonderment until by sound on the part of the lamb, and smell on the part of the mother ewe, her milk now heavy and wanting to be had, the two came together in the milling, bleating flock.

Then, chilled by the night breeze, still like a cowering thief, he would retreat into the night, glancing back once or twice at the many brightly lighted windows of the farmhouse. He felt, too, a strange, lonely warmness as he paused at the crown of the last hill.

Behind him there still came on the night breeze the faintest whisper of some mother sheep bleating for her lamb. Before him, far down in the hollow, the dim yellow light of a lamp came through the window from where it sat on the kitchen table. This made his loneliness warm and gave his step a firmness, with all the cowering gone. For soon he would be home. His father would say in his quiet way, "That was a good turn." And his mother would say, "Don't you want a piece of bread or somethin' before you go to bed?"

He would tell his little sister and brother how the lamb and the mother sheep found each other. And one of them would say, usually Sara, "I wish we could have a lamb of our own."

Now the boy was too happy to hurry. He had stood a long time at the crest of the slope. "Come on, Rowdy." He bent and tugged at one of Rowdy's ears lightly. "Next spring I'll teach you to help me find lambs when they're lost in fence rows and thickets."

Every year, Ollie Cantrell bought two lambs from Thomas Ruffner and raised them for meat. He let Aaron make pets of them, but it was sad for Aaron when they were butchered.

Chapter Five

The slope dropped sharply as it came to the creek bed. There, in the shade of the sycamore trees and the gorge which provided a channel for a hint of a breeze on an otherwise still afternoon, several small groups of Thomas Ruffner's Shorthorn cattle rose from the shade as the boy and dog came into sudden view at the top of the steep rise. Both boy and dog were as surprised as the startled cattle. Rowdy let out a clipped yelp and raced down the bank, where the cattle, after an initial moment of jumping and blowing, had formed a milling half circle between the boy and the fence. One or two cows with calves lowered their heads and blew threateningly at Rowdy as he jumped about too close to the circle.

The sudden deep, guttural, almost thunderlike lowing from the herd and the appearance of a head bowed to the ground, snorting with each step and pawing the earth, brought the boy up sharp. One of Thomas Ruffner's Shorthorn bulls, against which Aaron had been warned, was advancing upon Rowdy, who, though barking furiously, charging and darting, was slowly giving ground back toward his master.

Thomas Ruffner did not dehorn his bulls. If he had shown them at the county fair, leaving the horns might have been understandable. But since he didn't, and especially letting them run loose, his reasoning was difficult for anyone except Thomas Ruffner to understand. Perhaps these thick-butted, short horns, which grew horizontally from the head and whose points curved back toward the head rather than out and upward, did not look dangerous to the man astride his tall roan stallion.

To Aaron Skinner, measuring the distance he had to go to reach the safety of the fence on the other side of the creek bed, head and horns, dust and stones thrown up by pawing forefeet, the deep bellowing and terrible exhaling snorts, all presented a numbing, dreamlike horror. The boy's calls to Rowdy went unheeded. The round cobblestones of the creek bed made Rowdy's footing unsure. Several times he was sprawled among them and half hidden in the cloud of dust raised by the hot breath of the lowered head, its mouth dripping foam. And white half circles, set fixed above the eyeballs, which rolled from side to side following the dog, seemed to grow larger as the eyes narrowed.

The boy, at first concerned to save Rowdy, had fixed

his eyes upon a fallen sycamore branch, but the bull had advanced too rapidly. Now the branch was behind him. As he stooped to try to loosen a stone from the earth, Aaron's feet slipped on the steep, gravelly bank, and he found himself sliding into the dust cloud of the dilated nostrils, their raw linings pushed outward and fiery red.

Rowdy was still between the boy and the bull, but now the dog's movements were hampered by his attempts to avoid landing on his master as he darted from side to side as the massive head and horns swung and jabbed. The boy had ceased his yelling at the dog. Now his feet and hands stopped their frantic clawing to get a footing and a grip of the earth to push and pull himself back up the bank. A spasm of fear seized his body. The dust cleared, the dry heat cooled. The boy knew the meaning of the instant. The spasm passed in a second. The boy knew the awful, calming truth of the second: Aaron Skinner was going to die. It was from inside him. Not from his lips in agony, "I'm going to die," screamed or cursed. But a beautiful voice, whispering quietly, "Aaron Skinner is going to die."

People review their whole lives in a second's dying. Or they pick out a day or a moment and relive it. An aged man will be a boy again and call to his father across a field, "Wait for me, Father. The stones are hurting my feet. I can't keep up." An old lady will say to a playmate, "Give me my doll. I must hurry. Mother is waiting. She said to come at sundown."

And what thoughts and scenes, swifter than lightning, etched their picture lines on the boy's rather drab and colorless panorama of memory. For almost all his hopes had died before a boy's long day died — even as this day's hope and dream was dying in a dry gulch before a day's end.

The crowns of the hills and the sky rolled up and away before him. The hills, which had been his prison, whose shadows pressed down upon him, where he had carried his father's dinner pail, searched a lost lamb, or earned his bitter wage chopping the sproutland, now shone in different light. Too late he saw them as a place for a boy to run, to whistle to his dog or rouse an echo from a passing breeze.

And only now, closely passing in its wavy flight and pouring sweetness down from late summer's high-ceilinged sky, a meadow lark warmed his heart. It had been singing all his summers, but he had never listened. If he could catch a fragment of the song now, amid the bellowing snorts of death's hot breath and yelps of agony from Rowdy, mauled against the stony earth, how he would stand and hear the whole song and know the pattern of the flight if it could be again! And it would be, but he would not be there. Sara and Seth he wouldn't turn upon again and say, "Don't follow me, I have to take Pa's dinner pail." If he could now go back he'd call to them to hurry: "Hurry! I'll show you where the chipmunk gathers seeds and stores them in a hollow log, and a bobwhite's nest with eighteen eggs right on the ground and nothing bothers them."

Now Rowdy's up. The hide stretched over his meatless spine and ribs is bloody. But he is fiercer now. He's snapping at the livid red of the outturned nostrils and

46

the foaming mouth. His teeth snap together with the sound of hammers striking.

Faster than sunbeams flashing off a windowlight, thoughts flash in the boy's mind's eye. "How long will it be before somebody finds him?" The short-cut path on the other side of the fence was not too far away, but out of sight of the gulch where the boy lay trying to shrink into the bank, clutching the earth with his hands, digging in his heels so that he would slide no closer to the thrashing head and horns and the great, arched neck.

Ollie Cantrell, going to the store by the path, feeling his way with his cane, wouldn't find him. The cattle would move out of the shade to graze when the sun went down. And if Mr. Ruffner came riding to check his cattle, he'd see them grazing far from the gulch. Perhaps no one would find him for a long time, flashed through Aaron's mind. Maybe Mr. Ruffner, as the boy had seen him sitting on his tall roan stallion studying black wings circling above some hill or hollow, then finding a dead sheep or calf and sending Aaron's father to bury it. And the boy's father never letting him go, because "It'd make you sick," he'd say.

Mr. Ruffner would be mad, even if he was sorry, for Aaron was in a field where Mr. Ruffner had said, "Don't go." He would ride to find Jake Skinner. Then, above the rattle of the bit from the big roan's nervous champing, with his eyes going past Jake Skinner to the ground, he'd say, "I've got bad news, Jake. Your boy went in one of the fields he wasn't supposed to, after a stray dog I think he must have. Anyway, it's an awful thing, but they're both dead, him and the dog, down in the creek-bed gulch by the big sycamores. The ground is all pawed up, and they're awful mauled. Looks like the bull caught them up against the bank and they couldn't get away."

Rowdy will back no farther. His hind feet brush the boy. The bull has given up his forward advance and now weaves from side to side, arching the foam-spotted neck, horns almost on the ground, trying to hook the dog. Now Rowdy's wild snapping makes contact with the tender hairless strip of the bull's extended upper lip. His hound's jaws lock. But his hound's instinct to shake his prey is not necessary. The bull lets out a long bellow of pain, and now Rowdy is tossed from side to side with the speed of a whiplash. Now dog and bull's head are a blurred smear of dust and blood and foam. The muzzle skin of the bull begins to tear from the weight of Rowdy being tossed about. His sharp hound's teeth cut like pointed knives until they rip their way to the end of the muzzle. The dog flies through the air and lands by the side of the boy. The bull hesitates long enough to raise his head high in the air, curl his tongue over his bleeding nose, and lick it gently.

For a second the dog lies still. The breath has been knocked from under the loose hide and protruding ribs. "Dead like Amos" flashed before the boy. And another of those strange, sometimes weird and unexplainable memory pictures which unreel a life in an instant, when time is going out, came to the boy:

His little brother Amos had died with the whooping cough a long time ago, but he still remembered everything about it. Amos was five and he was seven. They both had it at the same time.

Their mother had moved their bed into the kitchen and kept the teakettle steaming all the time. And she mixed vinegar with the water in the kettle so the whole kitchen smelled like a cider mill. When the whoopin' was bad, she propped Aaron up in bed with pillows and fed him warm honey out of a spoon. His father walked in front of the stove with Amos over his shoulder so the steam came right up to him from the teakettle. When half the night was gone, Aaron would fall into a wheezy sleep still propped up, straining his eyes for one last look at his father holding Amos, and hearing, as sight and sound slipped into nothingness, the creak of the kitchen floor under his father's pacing up and down.

Then, one morning Aaron awoke whoopin' and choking with everything else still in the house except the teakettle steamin'. He thought Amos was better, sleeping by his side, with his head flat on the pillow, his back turned toward Aaron.

But when he turned to snuggle closer to his little brother, and touched him under the covers, Amos was cold, even with all the covers still tucked in around him.

"Amos, are you better? Are you warm enough?" Aaron asked quietly. But there was no answer or movement. Aaron bent over his brother and looked down into his face. Blood and phlegm had oozed out of one side of his mouth and stained the pillow. His eyes were open. Amos was dead.

Aaron watched in the numbed silence, disturbed only

by the teakettle steaming, as his father walked up and down again, holding the dead child in his arms. When he had done this until it was time for the village store to open, he gave the dead child to its mother and went away for help.

There was blood around Rowdy's mouth and slobbering, too, on the gravel and dust, almost just the way the phlegm looked smeared on Amos' pillow. It had been so long ago, with sister Sara only a baby and Seth not born. While his father had gone for help his mother sat close to the stove, moving back and forth on a cane-backed straight chair, pretending it was a rocker, pretending to keep his dead, cold little brother warm, pretending she was rocking him to sleep. And talking to herself in a hoarse voice, "God Almighty's lightnin' strikes when and where it will," and talking to little brother Amos with her mouth close to his ear, like she's whispering, "It's the Lord's doin', my baby, not none of mine."

Before the bull had licked the blood from his torn muzzle, Rowdy was on his feet, charging again with both bounce and bark. And in the time-defying panoramic recall which impending death was providing Aaron Skinner, his mother's words, "God Almighty's lightnin' strikes," pulled up one day from the several thousand which, passing without great variation, had added up to his young years — one day's sharp stab of memory and a message for the heart.

The boy had finished his dinner (midday meal) of sliced tomatoes, cold biscuits, and side meat. The woman, who had spread the table for Aaron and two younger children, pressed the lid on a half-gallon molasses pail and set it on the table before the boy. Picking up the empty plates and dishes from the table, she spoke to the two smaller children, "Get out of this hot kitchen and play in the cool shade of the porch."

"There ain't no place cool these days," the boy interjected, and added with a touch of bitterness, "Why ain't there no trees around our house like other peoples'? Ollie Cantrell has so many trees around his house that he's in the shade all the time."

"A blind man doesn't know whether he's in the shade or sunshine. Those trees were there when Ollie Cantrell was born blind and he's never seen them."

"He taps them with the broomstick he carries when he goes to the pigpen or the cowshed. And he always sets under the same one when he's making brooms or fixing split-bottom chairs. But why ain't there trees here?" the boy asked again.

"I guess nobody just never thought to plant some. And if they thought of it, they said it'll take too long for them to grow to do any good. Besides, our patch of ground is hardly big enough to get the pigpen far enough from the house to keep it from smellin' all the time. And the garden patch in between, and right up against the house. If there was any trees they'd shade the garden and hamper growin' things."

"The Keck place has locust trees on every side, four times higher than the house and chimneys, must be more than two dozen."

"Locust trees draw lightnin'. There ain't no use settin' and talkin' about what you ain't got." She showed her impatience by pushing the molasses pail closer to the boy.

"Your father will be famished up there in them dry hills. You get a fresh jug of water at the spring and git up there with it and his bread and meat. Don't let the jug touch the bottom of the spring. It's nearly dry and the water won't clear before suppertime."

"Our well's been dry for more'n a month, and Ollie Cantrell's still pumps without priming, and he doesn't even say save the rinse water for the hogs when I wash the milk pail. It's a pity somebody don't live in the old Keck house. With that big spring right down the bank from the back of the house, feedin' that whole cress pond, there's water enough to feed an army. If the Keck place was up here where we are at the head of the hollow, this wouldn't be called Dry Hollow, for that spring would keep the creek going the whole two miles to the main road."

"Stop dreamin' 'bout what ain't and git up the hill to your Pa. And don't dawdle up there if you can't help him with nothin', like pilin' brush. You've got stovewood to chop, water to carry, and redroot weeds to pull out of the turnip bed and potato rows for the hog before you go for Ollie's cow. Are you listenin' to me, Aaron Skinner?"

The boy had moved to the edge of the porch and was searching the sky for a cloud. "I'm listenin'. I was just thinkin' there might be a rain comin'. There's a ball of wool risin' above House Mountain."

"Tell your Pa not to stay up there with that ax on a hilltop if a storm threatens. Metal draws lightnin' in high places. And thinkin' about the big locusts at the

Keck place, the lightnin' sure did strike there aplenty."

"I never saw one tree struck."

"I didn't mean that kind of lightnin'. I meant another kind of God Almighty's lightnin', the puzzlin', mysterious kind."

"What kind?" the boy asked as though he hadn't heard his mother's last remark.

"What I mean about another kind of God Almighty's lightnin'? The kind that struck me with little Amos dyin'."

"Seems to me like God Almighty's lightnin' strikes the wrong people. Why don't it strike ole Tom Ruffner? He's the meanest man I know. I hate him so much that when I see him gallopin' his horse over the fields I wish it would stumble and he'd bust his skull against a rock or stump."

"That's an awful thing to say. You only a child and full of gall. Better not let your Pa hear you talkin' that way. You just say, 'Howdy do, Mr. Ruffner,' and nothin' more."

"I do," the boy answered with his voice still full of hatred.

"Be careful of snakes on the way up. This dry weather brings them out of the mountain searchin' for water."

The boy did not call back. He was well along the path that led to the spring. The spring was on Mr. Ruffner's land, but he didn't mind if the Skinners got water there. Aaron Skinner's father had worked for Mr. Ruffner for as long as the boy could remember.

Real bad trouble was what Sophie Skinner called the other kind of God Almighty's lightnin'. But sometimes she called the same trouble "the Lord's will."

Why did his mother have to mention all the things he ought to do but didn't want to? He had been thinking he'd hurry back from taking his Pa's dinner and water jug, beg Sara to pull the redroot weeds, save the wood and water for later, and hurry down to the big sycamore where the village boys played baseball. If he got there before their whole gang gathered he thought they'd let him play. Then he wouldn't have to sit on the roadside with Babe, the crippled boy, and watch, the way he always did.

He'd be right there when they finished playing ball, too, and went up Buffalo Creek to the swimming hole under the cliffs. He would walk right along with them.

When he tried to go after they were already there, they always came out of the water and threw rocks at him. He always planned to stand and fight back, but he never did. They were too many, and he was alone or had only Babe, the crippled boy, who walked with one foot turned sideways and dragging, and whose head was turned to one side and bent down on his shoulder. People said he had been injured at birth and wasn't very smart. But Aaron liked him for a friend.

Now Aaron hurried. He'd leave the redroot weeds and the wood chopping for later. He wouldn't offer to help his Pa in the hills. At the spring he held the water jug on its side with both hands to let it fill, careful not to let it touch the bottom and muddy the water, for it was very low and the stream was so small that it would take forever to clear. When the spring was full he could see himself in the water, and then he would start thinking about a lot of things and dreaming. And he could dream himself far out beyond the hills. Now with the water too shallow for him to see himself, he just counted the air bubbles gurgling from the jug as the water pushed them out.

His day ended with all his dreams escaped like the air bubbles. He saw himself lying down on his bed in the dark, hating that day as he had so many of his life. There came to him a quiet voice, which said, "Go back and say good night. You didn't say good night to your father and your mother. You didn't say good night to your sister and brother." And there came to Aaron Skinner an awful awareness of neglect of heart-life in favor of hand-life. He wished that he could do that day and many other days over. He whimpered to himself, "But I didn't understand." Somehow the boy understood now that all the beautiful, simple mysteries of life, like the sound of saying "Good night, Pa" or "Good night, Ma," he had missed, because all beautiful mysteries which are simple and not hard to understand come from the heart.

Now in his darting from side to side to escape the bull's once again lowered and swinging head, Rowdy actually gained ground, moving the bull back a few steps. Then with one lightnin' dash he turned and came to the boy, barking plaintively down into his face. Aaron knew now that his concern had been the dog's all the time. Rowdy was trying to save him. Was he saying now, "Scramble up and run. I'll hold the bull 'til you make the fence"? Why else would he be charging in with so much ferocity and renewed strength when only a second before, his body had been sprawled by the boy's side? And Aaron

Skinner had taken one of his hands from clutching the earth and put it gently on Rowdy's head, certain that they were about to die together.

Suddenly the boy knew why Rowdy had spared that precious second from the fight to bark down into his face. A new movement swam before the terrified vision of Aaron. Movement so fast that it was blurred. The bull was whirling round and round, almost as if he were trying to catch his own tail. His head was going from side to side as well as up and down, and the bellowing was a long-drawn-out rumbled cry of pain like the one which had shaken the earth when Rowdy's teeth tore into the tender lining of the bull's upper lip.

Rowdy was stretched across the swiftly moving head and horns. He looked almost comfortable for an instant. His teeth were clamped in the bull's ear, and a trickle of blood and foam was encircling one of the half circles of white which was all that showed of the bull's eye to the boy on the bank.

Falling, crawling, digging his feet and fingers into gravel, clutching stones in the creek bed, Aaron Skinner passed the whirling circle of bull and made it under the barbed-wire fence. The bull saw him and rushed to the fence, Rowdy still dangling on the shelf of the great, curved horns. Now the boy is on his feet, searching for a loose stone or club, calling to Rowdy to let go. Close against the fence the bull makes one last wild toss of his head and Rowdy's body is rubbed over the barbed wire. The barbs tear his hide, the pain is too much. He lets go his grip and falls just below the fence. In an instant the boy has the torn body dragged under the fence. The anger-blinded bull's great head crashes into the earth just where the dog's body had touched the earth. Aaron half drags, half carries Rowdy a short distance to the foot of the nearest sycamore tree. There, out of sight of the bull, they wait.

The bull tried his head against the wire once or twice, then gave up. He paced to and fro along the fence for a dozen times, then turned away. In a tall clump of milkweed on the far side of the creek bed he massaged his nose and his ear until the milkweeds were worn to the ground. The boy had seen his father rub a bleeding briar scratch with milkweed. He wondered how the bull knew it was good for whatever was hurt. Not until he had bathed his wounds with milkweed juice and turned back to join the rest of the cattle did Aaron speak to Rowdy, still on the grass, his torn sides heaving, streaked with blood, but his eyes open and soft, looking up into the face of his new master.

Aaron was too weak to move. He sat leaning against the tree, still stunned from his closeness to dying. He caught himself studying his hands and feet; they would move. He was alive. But the shock came back in waves of being sure and then wondering if they were both really alive. Seeing the bony, ribbed sides of Rowdy rise and fall in labored, painful breathing was the most beautiful sight in the whole world.

Over the dried blood and slobber, caked with dried earth, the boy rubbed the dog's head, and after a long time spoke quietly to him, "You saved my life, Rowdy. Now you look worse than ever. I'll love you forever." The boy felt his pocket. The collar was still there. Now he thought he'd exchange it for an even better one. He'd get Rowdy one that not only had brass studs but a shiny plate for Rowdy's name on it. He'd get Mr. Carter at the blacksmith's shop to stamp it on, and he'd pay him with money from the first coon hide he sold.

"It ain't much more than half a mile to Ollie's and I'll carry you in my arms like a sick child and you won't hurt a bit," the boy said to Rowdy as he got to his feet. But Rowdy was up at the first movement of his master. For the first time, Aaron noticed that Rowdy's right front foot was bloody, and on looking closely, found two toenails missing. Rowdy limped badly on this foot, but wagged his tail, licked his master's hand, and with turned-up eyes, moved along the path at his master's side. "If your foot hurts too much, you'll stop to lick it. Then I'll know I ought to carry you," the boy said, musing to himself, looking back one last time at the dry gulch.

The cattle had moved out to graze on the slope. At a distance they all looked the same, their heads moving gently in a rhythmic cropping of the grass and their tails keeping time as they beat flies from flank and belly. There was no sound except an occasional low, muffled call of a mother to her calf to come for milk.

Chapter Six

Since the short-cut path followed only a short distance from the creek bed, the boy turned aside to look at several spots where seepage springs kept little water holes going long after the creek was dry. He wanted to wash the caked blood and earth from Rowdy before he got to Ollie's. But there was no water to be found until he reached Ollie Cantrell's well pump.

Ollie was nowhere in sight. "We'll get you cleaned up before Ollie sees you," the boy said as the two quietly approached the well; then in a whisper added, "What am I saying? Ollie won't ever see you, but he can feel you."

Something from the boy's thoughts when he felt he was going to die came back to him now. Blind Ollie Cantrell had always been his friend. It had never bothered him when he'd said to Ollie: "Did you see how Tom Ruffner hit that horse over the head?" or "See them birds chasing that hawk over the treetops." He had never really bothered to think about how things might sound to somebody. Now he felt empty inside from just the feeling that his blind friend might have felt when someone carelessly said "see" to him.

Aaron lifted and lowered the pump handle very quietly. He filled Ollie's sprinkling can, wondering as he did how Ollie knew where the plant rows were to water them. He had never thought about this before either; he'd offer to water the garden in exchange for Ollie's letting him leave Rowdy there until he looked more like a fifteen-dollar dog.

When the can was full he poured it along Rowdy's back. Rowdy ducked and shook himself, but calmed down and wagged his tail when his master gently wiped him with the cloth Ollie Cantrell used to cover his pig feed to keep out the flies.

Rowdy had now had the second bath of his entire life, and both in the same afternoon. Aaron felt an unspeakable pride and a strange feeling that standing at Ollie Cantrell's kitchen door, as he had stood and knocked a thousand times before, was something to be glad about.

Ollie was his friend, but almost always Aaron had felt a twinge of resentment when he came to Ollie's, because he was coming either to do something for milk or money, or just simply to escape the loneliness which was forever gnawing at something inside him. Now he hoped Ollie would say he could leave Rowdy for a few days, but if he didn't, Aaron knew he would understand. He had been saved from dying; he was never again going to resent or hate anything that had to do with living. He was not even going to hate Mr. Ruffner any more. For Mr. Ruffner didn't ride down to the dry gulch when he saw buzzards circling and find Jake Skinner's boy and a stray dog. Jake Skinner's boy was alive, and a dog named Rowdy, no stray, was alive. The next time Aaron Skinner saw Mr. Ruffner riding his tall roan stallion he was going to say, "Howdy, Mr. Ruffner. It's a nice day today."

"I've finally bought my dog," Aaron said to Ollie as he opened the screen and felt his way to the edge of the stone step below the kitchen door. When he had seated himself on the stone, he said, "Bring him here."

"That's what I wanted to see you about," the boy said as he snapped his fingers and moved Rowdy toward the blind man. "He's awful skinny, and I paid fifteen dollars. I'll get an awful — " he was going to say "tongue-lashing from Ma," but he changed and said, "Ma and Pa will feel sorry that I didn't get much for my money if I take him home this way. I thought you might let me keep him in the cowshed a week or two until I'd fattened him up."

The blind man had felt along the saw-tooth ridge of Rowdy's backbone and rubbed his hand over the ribs. "He is a little thin. What color is he?"

"Blue Tick," the boy answered, "white with brownish-blue dots. Already trained for coons and a year old."

"Does he have a name?"

"Yes, I named him Rowdy. For he was rearing to get away from Matt Watts' place as fast as he could. My store collar is too big, but I'm goin' to take it back and get one that has brass studs and a name plate too."

"Rowdy is a nice name for a fast huntin' dog."

"I could work out what some milk for him would be. And I could bring biscuits and corn-meal mush from home."

"Do you think he'd whine and bark and disturb Mother? That's the only thing I'm thinkin'."

"Not if I tell him not to. And I'll walk him in the hills and be with him almost all the time."

"Let's go look for a strap in the cowshed that will fit him for a collar."

As the blind man and boy moved along the path to the cowshed, Rowdy walked between them, limping badly on the foot with the toenails torn off. The boy started to explain the limp and all that had happened with the bull. But he stopped short, remembering that Ollie didn't know Rowdy was limping. For a reason he felt but could not explain, Aaron had decided he would never talk to anyone about the awful seconds when he thought he was going to be killed.

The blind man directed Aaron to look along the wall behind the cow's stall, where a collection of tie ropes, halters, and straps hung on wooden pegs. When a strap the right length was found, the boy buckled it on Rowdy's neck and snapped on his chain.

"Put some hay on the grain-room floor. This will be the best place for him," Ollie said as he tapped out the spot with his walking stick. "But you don't want to tie him up yet; you'll want him to follow you to bring home the cow."

"No, he's got a foot that's a little sore. I won't take him with me for a few days." Aaron didn't want the village boys or the store loafers to see his skeleton hound either.

Rowdy seemed to understand that he was supposed to stay behind and not make any noise. He had been chained or penned most of his life. His wish to go with Aaron was expressed with a hurt look from eyes dropped to the bottom of their sockets. He gave a subdued whimper. Then he stretched his pained body carefully on the hay and bedded his head between his outstretched paws, his eyes fixed on his young master as he walked away with the blind man.

It was later than usual by the time Aaron Skinner had found the Cantrell cow, watched Rowdy drink his pan of warm milk from Ollie's pail, not Aaron's. Aaron had offered, hoping Ollie would say no. If he used part of his molasses pail he would have to tell his mother a lie or she'd know about Rowdy. He'd have to say he spilled some on the way. He'd never thought much about lying to Sophie Skinner to save himself from a tongue-lashing or having his ma put out with him. But Ollie's saying, "No, I've got plenty. I even give milk to the pigs. You save yours," had made the boy very happy. For that same feeling that was making him think differently about so many things made him feel he'd rather not lie to his mother.

"You can't carry corn-meal mush in your pocket," Ollie Cantrell called to him as he was finally on his way home. "And don't worry about it. We'll have him fattened up in a week so much he'll be too lazy to hunt."

The boy studied the late-summer sky as he walked along the road. Twilight was gathering. There were no dark wings circling the sky. The shadows were filling up the hollow from the bottom. There was still a crown of soft gold on the hills. It appeared eerie and gave the hills a mystery Aaron Skinner had never seen or felt before.

When he put the pail of milk on the kitchen table, Sophie Skinner said, "You're late!"

"I didn't mean to be," the boy answered.

"You never mean to be. That's all I ever hear. I say day after day, 'Get the stovewood in and the pig fed before your pa comes from work,' and every day it's the same." The woman's voice had lost its harshness and inclined to softness as she finished speaking. She was suddenly aware that there was something different about the boy.

After supper the boy sat out the twilight and nightfall on the porch. There was the usual talk of hard times and weather from Jake and Sophie Skinner. Fireflies gave sight to the night, and the boy caught one for his little brother when he asked him just once. The far-off, plaintive call of a whippoorwill gave sound to the dark distance beyond the hills. "Why do you hate the whippoorwill so much?" little Sara asked her brother.

"I don't," Aaron answered with a voice which bordered on sadness.

64

"You said just last night you did. I heard you," Sara challenged.

"It makes the night soft," the boy answered. "Maybe I heard it wrong before."

"You silly, it's the same all the time." Sara was used to arguing with her brother and wanted to continue. But her father interrupted the long silence which followed when Aaron did not fight back, "Seth and Sara, it's bedtime for you."

"I think I'll go to bed too," Aaron said. Halfway up the narrow stairs to his little room he stood for a long time in the dark. Then he called out, "Good night, Ma. Good night, Pa."

"The boy don't feel right; I think he's sick," Jake Skinner said to the woman after the footsteps were gone up the stairs.

"I thought that when he brought the milk," the woman answered. "But he ate a good supper."

The few days left of summer before school began were busy ones for Aaron Skinner. He spent as much of the day as he could with Rowdy at Ollie Cantrell's. After the second day he noticed a change in Rowdy's looks, he thought. Also, Rowdy no longer seemed starved. He refused the biscuits which Aaron saved from his own meals and slipped in his pocket for the dog. Ollie brought thick slabs of corn-meal mush from the kitchen at milking time. In Rowdy's pan it was covered with warm milk, right from the cow, and Rowdy licked the bottom of the pan so clean it looked like a mirror. Rowdy, seeing himself in the bottom of the pan, would growl deep down inside, and the hair on his back would stand up. Ollie and Aaron laughed aloud and teased him for trying to drive the strange dog from his feed pan. Ollie would say, "Let him have some feed, Rowdy. He's a skinny and starved dog, right out of Old Matt Watts' pigpen, like you."

Aaron rode to town with Mr. Hutton, the storekeeper, and exchanged Rowdy's collar for a smaller one. By paying twenty-five cents' difference he was able to get one with a name plate. The man at the hardware store had metal punches for all the letters of the alphabet. He asked Aaron what his dog's name was and then put the collar down on a small anvil and hammered ROWDY on the brass plate. Aaron had paid his last money for the collar. He was afraid the man would charge extra for the name. When Aaron asked him anyway, the man said, "No, glad to do it. And I'll bet Rowdy is quite a dog."

Rowdy's torn toenails healed. New hair began to grow back over the barbed-wire cuts. His ribs and washboard spine disappeared under a hide that began to look sleeker and sleeker each day.

The days and weeks which saw Rowdy change also brought a change in his master. Aaron Skinner now seemed to be in a hurry all the time. He hurried home from school. His hankering to loiter and play with the village boys no longer obsessed him. At school he hurried at his work. His teachers noted a change; the corners of the boy's mouth sometimes curled upward in a smile. At home he got in the stovewood and fed the pig without being told over and over. Sometimes he brought Ollie's cow an hour early. And always he filled in whatever time there was left over by walking and running with Rowdy — all Rowdy's lameness now gone.

Aaron had not mentioned to his parents his desire to have a dog since Rowdy had been at Ollie's. During the summer, when he was putting away his money in a cigar box, and counting it every night, he brought the subject up often, but always in the presence of both his father and mother. His father's quiet noncommitment tempered Sophie Skinner's harsh objection. Even so, her reaction bothered the boy. "We don't need no dog to whine for biscuits," she would say. "It's hard enough to get bread to feed the mouths we've already got."

The boy's father would say nothing. But Aaron felt that if he came home leading his dog his father would listen to Sophie for a while, then speak up and say, "Ah, let it stay. He's worked and bought it with his own money." His father would probably notice the new collar and chain and say, "That's a nice store-bought collar and a good chain, son."

So when the exciting day arrived for Rowdy to be shown as a sleek, well-filled-out, fifteen-dollar, one-year-old, trained hunter, Aaron waited at Ollie's until long after sundown. He wanted to be sure his father would be home from the fields.

The lamp was already lit in the kitchen and the door shut against the October cool. Aaron opened the door as wide as it would go, and stood framed in the light with Rowdy by his side. There was a moment of silence, then a squinting of eyes, and Sara and Seth jumping up to see who could get to the dog first. Both shouted as they went, "Aaron's got his dog!"

"Don't rush up to it like that," the boy's father said quietly. "It might not be used to strangers."

"I hope he ain't got no fleas. And don't let him in. A hound ain't no house dog." Sophie Skinner was interrupted by, "Wait now, Sophie," from the boy's father.

"He ain't got no fleas," the boy spoke up, moving inside to be near his father.

"Where'd you git 'im?" Sara asked.

The boy did not answer her directly. He was still talking to his mother. "He ain't been around any other dogs to get fleas since I bought him from Matt Watts several weeks ago. He was so poor I knew you'd make light of him and be mad, so I kept him down at Ollie's to fatten him up."

The man ran his hand over the dog's head and fingered the brass studs on the collar. "Nice collar, chain too. What's his name?"

"Rowdy."

"Why'd you call him that?" Sara asked in disgust. "I'd call him Sam. I think Sam would be a better name for a dog. My teacher read us a story about a dog named Sam."

"I don't care," the boy answered. "I named him Rowdy because he has a lot of spirit and was rearin' to get away from that awful pigpen where Old Matt Watts keeps his dogs penned. And his name is on his collar, too."

Rowdy responded to his new friends by wagging his tail and cocking his head this way and that to study the new situation. "He's a smart dog," the boy continued. "Ollie says he's almost human. Can understand anything you teach him. He never barks when he's chained up. Ollie taught him that, and to shake hands. And he comes

68

if you snap your fingers. Ollie taught him that, too. I knew you wouldn't let him in, Ma, so I've had a nice bed waiting for him under the porch."

"Oh, he can stay in a little while longer now," the man said. "He needs to get to know us all."

The days and weeks which followed were the happiest Aaron Skinner had ever known. The worry of keeping Rowdy a secret was over. The excuses for getting down to Ollie's house were no longer necessary. The change which had come over the boy after his experience with the bull in the dry gulch was even more pronounced now. The hills, which had been a prison and forbidding, were now heights for boy and dog to climb, a world where they could roam together. There, after school, with wood in, milk brought, and pig fed, Aaron Skinner watched Rowdy follow the best instincts of a hunter, racing in wide circles to discover a scent, standing on the highest point of a hill sniffing the air at all points of the compass.

At home Rowdy sat at the kitchen door, his ear cocked to hear his master's voice. When the boy went to his little room under the rafters, Rowdy would move around the corner of the house and take up his position below Aaron's window. Ollie Cantrell gave the boy an empty barrel, which he rolled home and made a house for Rowdy right under the window. When Rowdy climbed atop the barrel to be closer to his master, the boy stood the barrel upright and sawed a hole in the side for a door. Now when Rowdy jumped to the top of the barrel and stood on his hind legs, the boy could reach down and rub his nose. "A ladder with half a dozen steps," the boy said to Rowdy one night, "and you could sleep under my bed every night." And the very next night, with his master holding onto the collar, Rowdy climbed the rickety ladder a boy had hammered together that afternoon. Rowdy couldn't learn how to go down the ladder, but Aaron had a plan that worked.

"Aaron has taken to gettin' up early and startin' the fire in the cookstove," Sophie Skinner said to her husband after this had been going on for a few days. "Just says he likes to get up early. I thought he might be trying to slip meat to that dog, but I ain't missed none. I do notice some slabs of mush gone from the iron pot, but I won't say nothin' 'long as he comes down early and stirs up the fire. He sure is a different boy since he's had that dog; was different from the day he left it at Ollie's."

"He likes to get down early to see that dog," the man said. "Hates to leave him to even go to school. But he ain't missed the bus one time yet."

And Rowdy hated to see his master leave for school. But he submitted quietly to his chain and slept the day away waiting for the boy. In the afternoon, when the boy came in sight, the dog would lift his head high in the air and send a long mellow bark rolling through the hollow until it was softened and absorbed into music of promise for the boy quickening his step — a promise of raccoon hides to sell.

And the boy talked to Rowdy, bringing dreams ever closer and driving loneliness far, far away: "Just wait a couple more weeks. The frost has already taken the bitterness out of wild grapes and persimmons. Soon it will have those raccoon hides toughened up for winter and they'll be ready to bring a prime price. Then we'll be out every night. But you've got to be a good dog and be quiet and catch them on the ground. This year I ain't got no gun to shoot them out of a tree. Next year I'll have one. But if you catch them up a persimmon tree I can climb up and get them with a stick. Persimmon trees ain't very big. And if you get them in a grapevine that runs a fence or thicket, we won't have any trouble knocking them down with a long pole."

Then "God Almighty's lightnin' struck," as Aaron Skinner's mother said.

Late one afternoon boy and dog played their way up through Thomas Ruffner's hill pastures. Jake Skinner had said to the impatient boy, "Wait until November. That's when hides are heavy for winter." The boy wanted to remind his father that today was November first.

At the crown of the hill the boy called Rowdy and quickly snapped the chain on his collar. Approaching in the distance was the boy's father with Mr. Ruffner riding his tall roan horse with the nervous mouth. Mr. Ruffner was on one of his inspection rides, pointing here and there as he rode; the boy's father having to almost run to keep up with the impatient horse and man. Aaron Skinner knew that Mr. Ruffner had been known to shoot dogs caught in his sheep pastures. He wished he had not come to meet his father. He wished he could hide, but the land was open, there was no chance.

"Whose dog is that, son?" Mr. Ruffner asked above the clanking of the bit as the horse rattled it against its teeth.

Aaron Skinner thought he detected an unusual softness

in the man's voice, not like when he was ordering Jake Skinner to do or not to do something.

"It's mine," the boy answered. "I bought it with the money I made cutting cedars from your pastures."

"Get rid of it!" Now the man's voice was its stern self again. "You'd sooner used your money to buy a calf. I won't have a dog roamin' my sheep pastures at breeding time, scaring them out of breeding. And one dog in this hollow will be sure to attract more. You know the old sayin' 'Congregate like dogs.' No! Get that mongrel back where it came from. I had to shoot a dog that blind Cantrell had once. I'd have to do the same thing with that — that egg sucker and sheep killer, that's what hound dogs are good for."

"I could keep him on the chain," the boy said quietly.

The nervous horse rattled the bit and pranced. The man stirred in the saddle. "Tomorrow's Sunday. Get that mongrel out of this hollow before you come to work Monday." The man was now directing his order to the boy's father. But before Jake Skinner could reply, Thomas Ruffner slapped his horse's neck with the rein and was gone.

"If he hadn't run away, Pa would have told him," the boy forced himself to think as the two walked in silence over the crest of the hill. The dog frisked in and out between them, begging for the chain to be unsnapped.

At the crown of the hill the man stopped and stood for a long time. He seemed about to speak, and the boy waited. His father would speak and say, "I'll go and tell him in the morning that we'll keep the dog on our own land."

Below, already enfolded in the deep shadows of the vast hill pastures, which for a boy and dog had suddenly lost their lure, sat the whitewashed cottage of Jake Skinner. Its little square of earth, too small to grow a tree for shade in summer, was, both man and boy knew, too small to ever contain a boy and his dog. A world for a boy and a dog had to go on and on, across all the fields, over all the hills, and end where earth and sky ran together. Finally the man took up his slow, weary steps toward the house in the thickening shadows. Whatever thoughts held him standing so long, he kept to himself. The boy measured his slow steps behind the man, not by his side. Around them bounced Rowdy, with his spirit undampened. Halfway down the hill he cocked his head and studied his master. His master didn't snap his fingers or clap his hands and say, "Good boy, good doggie," to a frisky dog. Rowdy guessed he just didn't want to play.

Chapter Seven

The bitter cravings and unfulfilled dreams, which had not gnawed away inside the boy since Rowdy came into his life, and saved it, now brought back the "so much gall for a child" which Sophie Skinner had seen in the boy. The hills, which had brightened and opened up with a blue and sheltering solitude, giving the whole earth a new and sweet taste, now turned in an instant back into black, choking loneliness — mounds of gloom.

Aaron Skinner's whole insides swelled and burned with hate for Thomas Ruffner. His father wouldn't really have said to him even if he hadn't ridden away too quickly, "We'll keep the dog whether you like it or not!" Once before, Jake Skinner had quit working for Mr. Ruffner. Then he had to walk out of the hollow and three or four miles farther to a pick-and-shovel job on the road. But it was too far. So when he came back Mr. Ruffner had said, "Yes, you can come back to work, but the pay will be a dollar and a half a day, not two."

At the supper table Aaron kept his meat on the side of his plate. When he had satisfied his mother that he was too sick to eat, he carried his plate outside. Rowdy, who was used to corn-meal mush and hard biscuits, feasted on meat while the boy watched, too angry to cry.

After a long time sitting alone in the dark, the boy and dog came into the kitchen. "Tomorrow's Sunday, so you'd better take him then," the boy's father said.

That was all his father ever said. The boy wished he would say, "You didn't need it in the first place" or "We need other things besides a dog anyhow." If he said something like that the boy could hate him for not standing up to Tom Ruffner. Because he didn't say anything the boy felt sorry for him and loved him.

Sara and Seth went to the bend of the road with their brother and Rowdy as they started out for the six-mile walk to Matt Watts's. Sara tried to cheer Aaron up by showing him some of the different-colored leaves she gathered along the way. But Aaron Skinner did not want to be cheered up. He lashed his sister across the hand with the end of Rowdy's chain. The sharp ends of the twisted-wire, figure-eight links frayed her hand as if it had been scraped by a file or a piece of coarse sandpaper. Her pretty leaves fell torn to the ground, and she began to cry and suck her hand where blood oozed from long, red scratches.

"Go on back!" Aaron Skinner screamed at his little brother, who had not stopped with Sara. "And if you tell I hit you," he yelled back to Sara, "I'll git you sure when I come back. If I come back at all. I might not. I hate this holler and everything in it."

The world around Aaron Skinner was aglow with November's rainbow of color, which Sara had tried to show him in the colored leaves. But the world to the boy was a colorless hollow of gloom, where if a dream was brought to life something always made it die.

"I didn't even get to pet Rowdy and give him one last good-by. Aaron was awful mad," Sara said, more to herself than to her little brother as they walked toward home together.

"Does your hand hurt much?" Seth asked as Sara studied the purple welts rising between the oozing blood of the scratches.

"Awful. He swung that chain with all his might. Had to take it out on somebody."

"Yeah, but if they find out, he'll git it when he gits back."

"They won't find out. If they see it I'll say, I'll say — now what'll I tell? Too deep for briars, and the wrong side of my hand for fallin'. You can't bruise the back of your hand on rocks and gravel from fallin' if you're run-nin'. You bruise the front of your hand. I'll say — I'll say when Rowdy got to the bend of the road, with his chain on and not being able to bounce and run, he stopped dead still and just sat in the road lookin' back at home. He knew somethin' was wrong and wouldn't move. When I tried to help Aaron git him goin', he ran under the fence and pulled my hand against the barbed wire. That's what I'll say."

"That's a big lie."

"You shut up, Seth Skinner! I'll keep my hand turned palm up and maybe I won't have to say nothin'. I hope. But you're a tattletale. Watch this. See, I rubbed it on the fence. So I'll say I rubbed it on the fence, and stop at that. That won't be nothin' but the truth."

"They'll know it was more'n that."

"Just don't you start blabberin', Seth Skinner."

The six miles to Matt Watts's place were so much longer, seemed twice as long, than they had been when Aaron almost skipped the whole way a few weeks earlier with fifteen crisp one-dollar bills in his pocket, a new brass-studded dog collar in one hand and a bright five-foot chain, with a swivel snap, swinging in the other. On that trip he had hoped he would meet a lot of people and that they would stop and say, "Where's the dog? I see you have the collar and chain." He said his answer over and over to himself. "I've bought a year-old, trained Blue Tick coon hound that I bargained with Matt Watts for early in the summer. And I'm on my way to get him."

He wouldn't say anything about Old Matt not letting him take the dog until he saw all the money. Aaron had tried to pay him three dollars down and the rest later. Then he could have had Rowdy to go with him all summer. Old Matt had spat his tobacco juice in the dust right in front of Aaron and said a hateful thing, "You Skinners ain't got nothin' I could git my hands on if I didn't git my money. No, when you got fifteen dollars the hound is yourn, not before."

Now the closer the boy got to Matt Watts's place the more he dreaded it. Besides being crusty all the time, Sunday was the worst day for a visit to Matt Watts. Sundays Old Matt usually sat with a half circle of equally grizzly friends. There were usually half a dozen guns leaning against the porch posts or woodpile, depending on where the circle squatted. A stone jug was constantly being passed between them, each receiver performing a ritualistic movement of wiping the "other fellow's" tobacco juice from the mouth of the jug by rubbing it against his overall jacket sleeve. And in between it all there was a lot of cursing and loud laughing.

With this picture from past visits before him, Aaron Skinner practiced what he would say to Matt Watts. He also decided he would try to get him separated from his noisy cursing and guffawing friends, who always seemed to find fun in other people's troubles. They'd be some of the same ones who had laughed when Aaron had tried to get Rowdy for three dollars down.

He'd just say, "May I speak to you a minute, Mr. Watts?" And walk off just the way he'd seen the storekeeper do to Jake Skinner when he wanted to tell him he couldn't have another poke of flour on credit until he'd paid for the last one.

Four or five baying hounds took up positions at the end of the footbridge which crossed Buffalo Creek to a collection of unpainted buildings. A path led between them and numerous piles of old lumber, rusted wagons, manure spreaders, mowing machines, and hayrakes, to the house. The barking dogs at the bridge started a deafening chorus from a long, low building which had once been a hog house. It now housed Matt's "tradin' dogs."

Rowdy seemed as reluctant to cross the bridge as the boy. "Maybe I'll tell him you shouldn't be thrown back in with that fightin', snarlin' pack," the boy said as he stopped, knelt down, and held Rowdy's head close against him with one final hug before he rounded the buildings that hid him from view of the house.

Just as he had visualized, Old Matt and several friends sat on the porch, some on chairs, others squatting on the floor leaning against porch posts. All were positioned to get the Indian-summer sun, and all wore hats.

As Aaron approached, trying to steady Rowdy, against whom the free hounds had ganged up and were doing their utmost to chase him off the place, the men on the porch thought it was very funny. They laughed and slapped their knees. Those in the chairs rocked back and forth. One hissed, "Sick 'im, Mae Belle!" between the gaps in his teeth, then guffawed and added, "Ole Mae Belle ain't showed that much life since she rubbed her behind over that yellow jacket's nest five summers ago." Then they all joined in more raucous laughter.

Aaron Skinner thought how he'd like to have one of the guns leaning by the front door. He would point it slowly around the circle and say, "Now you have about two seconds to call these dogs off. And the next one who laughs will get this buckshot right in the belly!" But he stifled both his anger and fear.

When the fiendish laughter had died down and only intermittent barks from the one hound who continued to pester Rowdy made being heard less difficult, Aaron said, "Howdy, Mr. Watts. Could — ?"

But before he could finish, Old Matt spat halfway across the yard and pushed his hat back on his head. "How's the huntin', boy? Ain't that hound even better'n I said him to be?"

The boy's planned approach lost its well-rehearsed direction in the man's maze of questions. "You ain't spoilt him chasin' rabbits, have you? I guess you ain't. He looks like he ain't been runnin'. You've let him get fat and lazy maybe?"

Without further hope of getting Matt Watts alone, the boy scraped the toe of his shoe on the ground, and, studying the half circle it made in the dust to avoid the eyes of this terrible old man, he began in a voice that was almost a whisper. "I have to sell the dog back, Mr. Watts."

"What's that? Speak out! I can't hear for them damn hounds whining in the hogpen."

"Mr. Ruffner owns all the land. Says he don't want no dogs in the holler 'cause of his sheep grazin' and loose in the hills."

"That's a lot of nonsense and damn tomfoolery," one of Matt's friends, whom Aaron knew only as one of "the bootleggin' Meads" volunteered. "I've seen one hound or a whole passel keep a trail right through a flock of sheep and not raise a head from smellin' the scent to look at 'em. What the hell would Ruffner know about hounds? All he knows about is money and cheatin' somebody outa a fat calf."

This set off a series of stories about the stingy nature of Tom Ruffner, including the fact that his two sons had left home to work in the paper mills because he wouldn't pay them a living wage. Old Matt even said that he'd always heard that Ruffner got his wife, who had been a Lowman, when her father didn't pay for a cow he bought from Ruffner. The cow died before Ruffner came to take it back, so he took Lowman's prettiest girl for the debt. He had five. And even the prettiest wasn't much to look at.

While all this was going on between Watts and his friends, Aaron waited. When there was finally a pause for the passing of the jug, he spoke up. "When I bought Rowdy, Mr. Watts, you said if you kept him 'til huntin' season you could get twice what I paid. But all I want is my fifteen dollars back. And now it's hunting time and you can sell him for a better price."

Now there were great guffaws from all except Matt Watts. "Boy," he began, and spat much farther across the yard than before, "I sold you a dog. I got a whole hogpen full of dogs to sell. I ain't buyin' no damn dogs right now, and won't be for quite a while, I guess."

Aaron Skinner had planned on the long sad walk that he would try to convince his father to let him buy a secondhand .22 rifle and some steel traps with the fifteen dollars he would have for Rowdy. The dream of raccoon skins to sell he kept alive. He could trap and shoot them. "Would you have a secondhand .22 rifle and some steel traps you'd trade me?" he asked, and saw instantly that Matt Watts's rigid posture and boot heels thumping the floor made it the wrong thing to have asked.

"No, by God! I ain't got no gun to trade. What the hell would you do with a gun?"

The boy knew this question was not meant to be answered, so he kept quiet.

Matt Watts turned to the man whose last name Aaron knew as Mead. "Give me two dollars 'til I git my money poke from the kitchen cupboard when we go in," Old Matt growled.

With the money in hand Matt Watts rose from his chair and approached the boy. He shook the two one-dollar bills right in front of Aaron's eyes with one hand. "Here! God dammit! Now git!" At the same time his other hand jerked Rowdy's chain from the boy, tearing a gash between Aaron's thumb and forefinger and tearing the back of Aaron's hand. In the struggle to hold Rowdy when the other dogs had attacked him, the boy had wrapped the chain around his hand. The boy was jerked so hard he almost lost his balance and fell. His wild staggering to stay on his feet was very amusing to Matt's friends. They all laughed heartily. One started a second round of laughter when he said, "Why that boy can dance a real jig. And looka there. Somebody throwed two dollar bills at him for his dance."

Now amid wild laughter from the porch, Matt Watts

dragged Rowdy to the hogpen. He kicked two or three baying hounds, who tried to escape, then kicked Rowdy into the howling mass and slammed the door.

Matt Watts returned to the porch, cursing to himself as he went. "A man oughta never have no dealin's with poor white trash like them god-damn Skinners," he said as he took his seat and reached for the jug.

Aaron Skinner did not "git," as he had been ordered. Still sucking the blood that oozed from the tear between his fingers, he approached the porch steps. He was no longer hopeful. He was no longer afraid. A resolved anger now occupied his whole person. He had been called poor white trash when he first started to school. And when he asked his mother why, she had said, "It's no sin to be poor and there's nothin' one can do about bein' poor. But we ain't trash. We're clean and we keep our word. We pay our debts, but sometimes it takes us longer."

Now Aaron Skinner stood white and still. Only one or two of Matt Watts's friends continued to chuckle to themselves. The boy stepped slowly back to where Matt Watts had thrown the two dollars at his feet. He stooped and picked them up. Then he moved back to the edge of the porch and looked straight up at Matt Watts. He could scarcely get his voice above a whisper, but he was heard.

"I'm poor, Mr. Watts, but I'm honest. I could'a said Rowdy wouldn't hunt coons. You said you'd take him back if he didn't. I'm honest, Mr. Watts. So don't you call me trash. And I want my collar and chain."

"Git it! But you better not let any of 'em damn hounds

out. Then git over that footbridge and never set foot on this side agin."

The boy turned and walked toward the hogpen. Loud guffaws now followed him. "He'll sure have some damn picnic wading in what's left of butcherin' offals and dog manure," Matt said.

But the boy did not have to go inside. He cracked the door, spoke Rowdy's name, and one nose quickly pushed through the crack. The boy unbuckled the brass-studded collar of which both he and Rowdy had been so proud. He opened the door far enough to hold Rowdy's head close against him and rub his long silky ears one last time.

Without looking again toward the house, he crossed the footbridge. On the other side he knelt at the edge of Buffalo Creek to wash Rowdy's chain. It had been dragged through the filth of the pen, smelled terrible, and was caked with dirt. He also washed the dried blood from the back of his hand.

He could hear the loud guffaws and the intermittent baying of one lone hound as he turned toward home. He was sure that one voice belonged to Rowdy. Since the ramshackle barn and sheds shut out a view from the porch, he stood where he couldn't be seen and listened 'til the lone baying stopped.

He didn't want anyone he might meet along the road asking, "What you doin' with an empty dog collar?" So he rolled it up and put it in one pocket of his new winter corduroy jacket; the chain he put in the other.

85

Chapter Eight

The boy stood in the road, blowing on his smarting wound. He studied the road toward home, then turned his eyes in the other direction. How could he go home, he thought, and say, "Old man Watts was half drunk and didn't give me back but two dollars of my money"? Maybe he would take the road that went in the direction away from home. He would just walk and walk until nobody he saw would know him and he was lost in the mountains. Then he'd sit down by a big rock or crawl in a cave and go to sleep and die. He'd rather be dead anyway. And now he gave voice to his thoughts, "Cause my hand is hurtin' somethin' awful."

"But I'll go," he said aloud as he finally moved, turning his slow steps homeward. The feeling from the awful moments, with the bull's hot breath measuring the seconds left of life, came over him. The quiet of the shadow of a sheltering rock or a dark cave lost their appeal. Whatever plans he had of dealing with Matt Watts — his fifteen dollars in his pocket or a .22 rifle and a half dozen or more steel traps — as he had come this way before, were now shattered. He felt the two dollar bills in his pants pocket; he hated them. He wished he had disobeyed his mother and gone to see Ollie Cantrell the night before. His mother knew he wanted to ask Ollie if he'd keep Rowdy. He would stop at Ollie's a long time on the way home.

He had planned to get back to the Dry Hollow Road long before church was out. He didn't want to meet anybody on the way. But he had taken a long time going, and now he had no heart for hurrying. The morning was used up before he had gone very far. Halfway to the village he met the first people on their way from church. He felt his jacket pocket. Rowdy's collar was still neatly rolled up, none of it showed. He didn't want some kid to see the bright studs sticking out and say, "What's that in your pocket, a dog collar?"

He need not have worried. The people dressed in Sunday clothes hardly noticed him at all. A woman said, "Good morning," and Aaron said, "Howdy." Then he heard them talking about how beautiful the day was, and the pretty hills and mountains, all gold and red with fall colors.

A little farther on his way he saw old Mrs. Withers coming toward him, wearing her black Sunday hat and pecking the ground with the umbrella she always used as a walking cane. Aaron slipped under the fence and went behind Ike Eastman's deserted house. The half-open back door gave him a spooky feeling, but he'd almost risk seeing the ghost of Ike Eastman rather than face Mrs. Withers. If he stayed on the road, she would point her umbrella at him and say, "Now, Sonny, you haven't been to church and Sunday school. Shame on you."

He wasn't about to tell her he had just lost the one thing in the world that he loved most. And neither would he tell her that he didn't like to go to church and Sunday school anyway, because he didn't have any Sunday shoes and nobody else wore everyday shoes and khaki pants to church. Everybody but him wore a whole gray, or brown, or mostly dark-blue suit, and polished, low quarter shoes.

Aaron moved along the back of the house, careful not to trample some chrysanthemums blooming in a tangle of weeds. A drawer, pulled from a desk or cabinet, held the door ajar. Inside, the floor was strewn with pieces of furniture, paper, clothes, even the pictures taken from the walls. Here and there holes had been chopped through the partitions from one room to the other. The boy moved the drawer and quietly closed the door. He felt better with the door closed.

He heard Mrs. Withers' umbrella pecking the road at even intervals. He held his bruised hand out in the warm November sun. He studied the bank that ran down from the back of the house to the edge of Buffalo Creek.

Somewhere right along the edge of the bank they had found Ike Eastman lying, his head over the bank in a little pool of water. First it had been said up and down the creek that he had drowned. But when the coroner heard that Ike was considered sort of strange and was often made fun of and pushed around by the Meads and Wattses from upper North Buffalo, he held up the funeral and had an autopsy done. Ike Eastman's stomach was full of rat poison.

Aaron wondered exactly where along the bank they had found the body. He slipped to the corner of the house and looked toward the road. Mrs. Withers' umbrella was no longer making its rhythmic pecking on the road. Perhaps she was gone. Aaron had a creepy feeling and wanted to get out of there. He peeked around the side of the house. Mrs. Withers was standing in front in the middle of the road, looking from corner to corner and up and down as though she were certain she had heard something, or knew someone was there. After Aaron had watched her for a while he decided she was just thinking about Ike Eastman.

Isaac Eastman had lived alone. He had worked at the pulp and paper company over the mountain until he had been crippled in a wood slide from one of the giant pyramids of pulpwood. He had walked the twenty miles at the end of each week's work to enjoy his neat house and garden. Aaron Skinner had seen him dressed in a Sunday suit even on Saturday at the country store. The boy had dreamed of the day when he would be old enough to get a ride over the mountain on the bakery truck and hire out at the pulp mill. Then he would have a pocketbook that unfolded like the one Ike Eastman had, with one section for greenbacks and one for silver.

Ike Eastman was the only person who had ever called Aaron mister. Once at the store he had said to the boy, "How many brothers and sisters do you have, Mister Skinner?" When Aaron answered "two," Ike said to the storekeeper, "Give me fifteen cents' worth of peppermint-stick candy in three pokes." He gave the three bags to Aaron, saying as he did, "One for you, one for sister, one for brother."

The Meads and their North Buffalo friends had started trouble for Ike "just because he's too good for them to understand and easy to get at," Ollie Cantrell had said to Aaron once. "They don't have to go out of their way much to yell their threats as they pass. It all started over nothing," Ollie said. "Ike saw one of the Mead girls standing in the road admiring the flowers along his path. He asked her if she would like to see his garden at the back of the house. Just when they were coming back to the road a few minutes later, someone passed. Evil minds started a rumor that there was 'sumthin' goin' on there.' From that time on, the Meads pecked away at Ike like a coop of chickens after a runt."

Aaron peeped around the corner of the house again. Mrs. Withers was still standing in the road. He went back and sat down and leaned against the back of the house. He wondered why Ike Eastman had killed himself. He had heard one story from Ollie, but at the store he had heard another. There he had heard men say that Hard Times was the reason. They said Ike had money in the Mountain National Bank that went busted. They said when Ike heard that the President of the bank had shot himself, it started him thinking that if things was so bad the bank President killed himself, there wasn't much chance for anybody else. "Ike never kept a gun, 'cause he wouldn't harm a flea," they said. "Why he even tried to doctor crippled birds and animals and raised baby squirrels that had blown out of a tree in a storm."

The sun felt good on Aaron's bruised hand. It made his eyes heavy. It must have been terrible to take rat poison to kill yourself, the boy thought. It was the kind of rat poison that advertised on the box that rats won't die in the house and make an awful smell. They would go in search of water and die outside.

"That's why they found him on the bank," Aaron had heard the men at the store say. "He had mixed the rat poison with water and drunk it. Then, as it took effect, he just went out of his head and couldn't get enough water out of a dipper. So he tried to drink the creek dry."

Aaron Skinner thought it was the first reason that had caused him to kill himself. After all, there was the story that Ike had more money than what he lost in the bank. And Aaron understood what it was like to be picked on — "pecked at," as Ollie called it. Aaron had seen Ike take out his folding pocketbook and throw a dollar bill on the glass candy case to pay for fifteen cents' worth of peppermint-stick candy to give away and then not even count his change. This wasn't Hard Times.

Hard Times was what happened to Aaron Skinner all the time — like his father giving him a gentle tug on the shoulder when he'd stand looking in the candy case. Like wearing everyday shoes on Sunday and having people laugh. Hadn't he seen Ike Eastman wearing a Sunday suit on Saturday and not even going somewhere? No. It was the Meads' taking his front gate off the hinges and throwing it in Buffalo Creek, stuffing rags in the pipe that brought water from his spring, and throwing a dead skunk on his roof, and always yelling threats when they passed his house drunk in the night. Ollie was right. They drove him to it.

"An awful way to die," the boy said to himself. He heard the peck-peck-peck of Mrs. Withers' umbrella as she went on her way.

The sun was warm on his bruised hand. He liked the quiet of Ike Eastman's deserted house. He studied the bank of the creek, thinking he might walk down and see if he could find the likely spot where Ike, crazy with thirst, had stooped to drink his fill. But suddenly the creepy feeling he had felt at seeing the half-open back door came back to him.

He rounded the house quietly and began to crawl through the barbed wire at the end of the dooryard. Someone had thoughtfully nailed up the gate.

Maybe Ike did it just before he died, the boy thought, to keep people out. But then how did they carry the body out when they found it? "Lifted it over the fence I guess," the boy said aloud.

93

Aaron was halfway through the fence when the sound of a car came to him. In his haste to hide again, his jacket caught and ripped on the wire. It was his new school jacket. It was the first corduroy one he had ever had, like most of the other boys at school. He had always had just plain overall. This one he had bought himself with the money left over from cutting cedars from Mr. Ruffner's pastures after he had paid for Rowdy. He had wanted to buy a gun with the money, but his mother had said, "Wait 'til next year."

Now going home would be worse than ever, he thought as he ducked back behind the house. He would have to say he didn't get the money back for Rowdy. Sara probably had told he had hurt her hand. And now his mother would be hoppin' mad because he had torn his jacket.

But most of all he dreaded going home and not finding Rowdy there. It would be like coming back from the graveyard after they had buried Amos. He would think he heard Rowdy whine at the door, and even though he'd know he wasn't there, he'd get up and open the door. Just the way he used to wake up in the night thinking Amos was still beside him in bed. When he was wide awake he'd know he wasn't there, but he'd turn over and feel Amos' pillow where his head should be anyway.

The car that came into view was Mr. Thomas Ruffner's blue Hupmobile sedan. Seeing him only added to the empty, hopeless feeling that made Aaron empty and sick inside.

There might be other people coming along; he would wait until he was sure. He stretched his tired body —

tired from "heart hurt," as his mother would say. He lay with his head propped against the weathered boards of Ike's deserted house. The chill he had felt at seeing Thomas Ruffner, dissolved in the soft warmth of the Indian-summer sun.

Thomas Ruffner always rode alone. His wife didn't go to church, and he never offered anybody a ride. Aaron had even seen him pass Mrs. Withers, hobbling alone, and not offer her a ride. Just leave her coughing in a cloud of dust he left behind him. His Hupmobile sedan had cellophane curtains in the top, which rolled down like window shades. This was the biggest car all up and down Buffalo Creek.

Almost everybody else had cars which had to have curtains snapped on when it rained. Most of them were Fords and painted black. The storekeeper had an Essex touring car besides his pickup truck. The preacher had a Flint, but it was black, too, and not nearly as big as Mr. Ruffner's Hupmobile. There were only a few people left who didn't have a car. At school this was something that could be used to belittle and hurt. "Your parents don't even have a car" was meant to degrade and sting. It did sting, and it hurt, but Aaron Skinner never let it show. Some people fought back. He wished he could, but he always got weak inside and slunk away feeling ashamed and hating himself. The only car he'd ever ridden in, not counting the school bus and the storekeeper's pickup truck, was the preacher Mr. Dudley's Flint sedan. He had ridden a lot in the storekeeper's pickup truck.

The sound of Mr. Ruffner's car had been gone a long time. Even the cloud of dust it had raised had settled.

95

The boy raised his hand to swat at a fat housefly, which, warmed by the sun, had come from behind the boards. The tear between his thumb and forefinger opened and began to sting. He sucked away the new blood that began to ooze from it. His thoughts of a world with people like the pleasant man at the creamery and the storekeeper were now replaced by darker thoughts: Rowdy, who loved to stretch himself in the sun, now shut up in a dark and dirty hogpen, cowering in some corner with his tail between his legs, his spirit broken, trying to understand why his young master had deserted him. The boy turned on his side. He blinked his watery eyes. He pulled his knees up against his body as though he were in great pain. The sun dried the tears which hung in the corners of his closed eyes. The sound of Buffalo Creek moved farther and farther away until there was nothing but quiet, and a boy asleep in November's Indian-summer sun.

Chapter Nine

The boy jerked in his sleep so much that the late-summer fly gave up buzzing around his head and crawled back under the weathered boards of Ike Eastman's silent house. In his sleep the boy fingered the dog collar with the brass studs and the name plate with Rowdy's name on it.

He was about to rise and be on his way when, in his dream, he looked down the bank. There, on the other side of Buffalo Creek, sat Ike Eastman. Aaron Skinner knew it was in the middle of the week, but Ike was dressed in his whole suit with a vest. He motioned to the boy and called in a high-pitched voice which was not the voice Aaron remembered, "Come over, Mister Skinner. I've been watching you. You've been having a bad time. You almost got killed by a bull a few months ago. You were wrong to be so scared. Dying is better than living. Over here there's nobody to pester you. Just take the dog collar you have in your pocket and buckle it around your neck. In the shed off the kitchen of my house there are some hooks in the ceiling where I used to hang meat to cure. Stand on a chair, snap the dog chain on your collar, then hook it up tight over the hook. When you've done that, take one foot and kick the chair away and you'll be right over here with me the next second."

Now the dream changed. Aaron Skinner could only be saved if he got back to Rowdy and put the collar on him. If he got the collar on Rowdy, he couldn't use it to hang himself.

He ran all the way back to Matt Watts's place until he came to the footbridge. Then he crept carefully from one building to the next so Matt and his friends wouldn't see him. He was almost to the hogpen when the loud talk from Matt and his friends came to him as he ducked behind the corner of the woodshed.

"Why, he couldn't gone more'n a few hundred yards, his hind end was so full of buckshot it would serve like a vacuum to suck in the dust behind it." It was Lon Mead who was speaking.

"Hell!" cut in Matt Watts, "you stirred up the dust ten feet behind that damn dog. But who'n hell would ever thought he could climb up the cracks in them boards and jump out that peak? Jesus Christ! That's ten feet off the ground. Hell! I didn't even think a cat could climb that damn wall."

"What the hell you mean I hit ten feet behind that damn dog? I tell you I plugged his behind with buckshot. You just, by-God, wait here and I'll show you." Lon Mead had risen from his chair and was staggering right toward the woodshed where Aaron was hiding.

The boy tried frantically to unbuckle the collar from around his neck. Without knowing what he was doing, he had put it on while he was listening to Ike Eastman calling to him from the other side of the creek. Now he not only was wearing Rowdy's collar, but he was changing from a boy into a dog. He looked like Rowdy. Lon Mead was staggering toward him with a shotgun in his hands. Aaron crouched down on his hands and knees behind two or three large chunks of firewood, but they were not big enough to hide him.

But Lon Mead was very drunk and passed without seeing him. As a matter of fact Lon didn't even see the footbridge. He missed it and stumbled into the creek.

The boy still couldn't get the collar unbuckled, but he didn't look like a dog to be shot at any longer. He was standing up, well out of sight of Matt Watts and his friends, who had come down to drag Lon out of Buffalo Creek.

When they had laid Lon in the sun to dry and gone back to the porch, the boy slipped from his hiding place, crossed the footbridge, and began to search for Rowdy in the weeds and fence corners. He had climbed up the wall of the hogpen, using the cracks between the boards for a ladder, just the way Aaron had taught him to climb the ladder from the top of the barrel to his window. But now he was shot, and probably dead in a fence corner, or maybe dying. The collar was choking Aaron, but he walked faster and faster. Rowdy was waiting for him behind Ike Eastman's house.

Now he was there, but no Rowdy. "He's over here with me," the wind-strained voice of Ike Eastman called from across the creek. "Lon Mead shot him. He's waiting for you. Come on over before he strays off."

"Yeah, but if I do it here they might not find me for a long time. I don't wanta be like old Mrs. Keck. You know the story; somebody's always telling it around the stove at the store on a winter night. When she died they didn't find her for so long that her cats had started to eat her."

"That don't make no difference over here, not a particle of difference," Ike Eastman insisted.

"Anyway, I know a better place: the beams below the hayloft in Ollie Cantrell's cowshed. And Ollie's my friend; he'll find me in no time."

The collar was still very tight on the boy's throat, but he climbed the fence, ready to start for Ollie's cowshed. Ike Eastman had gotten up from where he sat on the other side of Buffalo Creek and was crossing toward the boy. His brightly polished Sunday shoes touched the stones which rose above the water. Just when he got to the spot where his body had been found in the water, he got down on his hands and knees and stooped to drink, calling to Aaron as he did, "Go in the kitchen and bring me the dipper; I'm awful thirsty."

But Aaron was over the fence and running. Before he rounded the bend in the road toward the village, he looked back. Ike Eastman was standing in the middle of the road with a Blue Tick hound by his side. The hound looked like Rowdy. But Aaron did not go back.

Near the intersection of the Dry Hollow Road and the road through the village, some strange people were gathered at the corner of Thomas Ruffner's land. The boy slipped through the fence and crossed the fields above the old Keck place in order to avoid them. Just as he was passing the upright tomb of old Mrs. Keck, which he had never done before, the front of it opened and a trim little lady with solid white hair, dressed in very old-fashioned clothes, stepped out and stood directly in the boy's path. Aaron was surprised, but not the least bit scared. He felt very comfortable in her presence and showed none of his timidness, but directly asked her a question as if she were sure to know.

"Who are those strange people gathered at the corner of Mr. Ruffner's field? I didn't want to go past them, so that's why I cut across the field."

"They're burying Thomas Ruffner, owner of my former fields. He liked my original idea of being buried standing up so he could look back on the hills he owned. But he'll be sorry." The woman's voice was soft and musical. There was not a single rasping sound that sometimes accompanies old age.

The boy wanted her to talk some more. "How did he die?" the boy asked.

"Went mad, riding over his hills day and night looking for the ghost boy and dog. Day and night he heard the dog barking among his sheep, but could never catch up with it.

"It was all inside him. It was his conscience. You see, after he caused you — "

"You know who I am?" the boy interrupted.

"Oh, yes! You're Aaron Skinner. You hanged yourself with your dog's collar and chain after Thomas Ruffner made you take back your dog. It's been five years. For three years Tom Ruffner rode the hills. He was always hearing your hound bark. He was always seeing you just go out of sight over the crown of a hill. He wore out his big roan stallion galloping to catch up with your ghost. Then, after three years, he went mad and they shut him up in the state asylum. There he died after two years. Never stopped calling for his gun to shoot the dog that was chasing his sheep."

"Then where have I been all these five years?" the boy asked, looking around him.

"There are no years here," the woman replied; "an instant and forever are the same. On earth I thought only of the harvest I could gather from my fields and hills. Now I am doomed to see forever all I missed in life — the heart of the fields and hills. For the harvest has no meaning here unless one understood the heart of the earth from which the harvest came. That's why Tom Ruffner will be sorry he liked my way of being buried. He wanted all his lambs. He never offered you an orphan lamb. He wanted all the fields and the hill pastures. He never knew the heart of the hills or heard their pulse beat. Now he is doomed like me to see forever all that was meant to be enjoyed on earth, all he missed to fill up his barn lot with fat sheep and cattle from his hill pastures, what he was blind to, measuring his grain from the thresher, never seeing it wave as a sea of gold in a June breeze, making the earth beautiful, before the reaper came."

"But I don't understand why you're telling me all this. I almost never got anything I wanted," the boy said with a slight hint of bitterness in his voice.

"That's why I'm telling you," the woman said as she took a step backward as if to return to her upright tomb. "You can still go back and want the right things."

"How can I go back? You said it's been five years," the boy asked frantically because the woman had taken another step backward and was now inside the tomb.

"Unbuckle the collar. It's choking you. You have been halfway. When Ike Eastman called, you didn't cross over like he wanted you to. If you unbuckle the collar you can go back if you make a promise."

"I'll promise! What's the promise? Will Rowdy still be a ghost dog? Can he go back?" The boy ran all his questions together, for the front of the tomb was slowly closing.

"The promise is easy. All you have to do is remember to still hear the water murmuring and laughing over the stones after the creek has dried up. And when you lie on the burnt crust of drought-dead earth in August you must remember the soft velvet green of April. You must look at the hills and sky together, the sky coming down to meet the hills instead of the hills rising starkly against the sky. Then you'll know that the hills have a heart. But the most important part of the promise is this: never let your tears fall to earth. They turn the spot where they fall into a salty desert where nothing grows. So whenever you have to shed tears, turn the corners of your mouth up to catch them as they run down your cheeks."

"But what — ?" The boy did not get to finish his question. With a loud bang that shook the earth beneath his feet, the crude concrete door of the tomb closed.

Chapter Ten

Aaron Skinner was awakened by the banging of Ike Eastman's kitchen door against the bureau drawer. The sun had disappeared behind a heavy gray sky that can shorten a November day. All the Indian-summer warmth was gone. Aaron was shivering in the November chill, and his teeth chattered. He swallowed to make his teeth stop chattering and his throat felt sore. He put his hand in his jacket pocket and felt Rowdy's collar.

Now he was wide awake and frightened. "What an awful, awful dream," he whispered, looking up and down both sides of Buffalo Creek. "He was right over there." The boy continued to speak half aloud to himself. "I hope Rowdy didn't get shot. I'll catch it if I don't get home fast."

It was late. Aaron could have saved time by taking a short cut through the fields behind the Keck house. But the square cement tomb, standing at the highest point of the land, dissuaded him. He kept to the road.

By the time he left the main road and turned in at the hollow road, it was almost dark. He hurried past the old Keck ruins at a fast walk on tiptoe, looking back over his shoulder at almost every other step. The November rains had not come, so the creek was still dry. He thought of his strange dream and the promise to hear the water running over the rocks when the creek was dry. He listened. Sure enough, there it was as plain as anything, the gurgle and muffled splash of water around and on the mud-caked stones.

He was in sight of the light in Ollie Cantrell's kitchen window when suddenly he froze in his steps. At the same time, he felt an irresistible urge to take Rowdy's collar from his pocket and look at it. He had heard the deep, prolonged bay of a hound. It came from the hollow and sounded to the boy like Rowdy's bark. "The ghost dog! I'm dead. I'm a ghost too," the boy said aloud as he fingered the dog collar.

On the chill November breeze the voice of the dog came again. The boy felt his other pocket. Rowdy's chain was still there. The rim of the moon rose above the hills as the boy stood listening. "She's right," he said aloud, "the sky comes down and lights up the hills; the hills don't go up and darken the sky. If I'm alive, I'll keep all her promises."

Ollie Cantrell opened the kitchen door just enough for a thin strip of yellow lamplight to escape and run across the path into the garden. "I thought maybe Ma didn't send Sara for the milk," Aaron said. Sundays he didn't have to bring the cow. People were asked to keep them in so they wouldn't mess up the churchyard and get in the cemetery when the churchyard gate was open for people coming to church.

Ollie threw the door wide. "Where have you been all day? There's been all kinds of trouble and excitement around here. And your Pa went all the way to Matt Watts's looking for you. He was worried after he heard what really happened that some harm might have come to you, too, or you might have brought harm upon yourself. He had that feeling, he said."

"I hid behind Ike Eastman's old house while people were passin' from church. I fell asleep in the sun and slept 'til the sun went down and the November chill woke me up with a sore throat. I hadn't slept much last night worryin' about havin' to git rid of Rowdy."

"You musta been tired, to sleep through the sheriff's car and everybody racing by. And they had you for dead."

"What happened, what'a you mean?" Aaron interrupted as Ollie motioned him in and lowered his voice.

"Lon Mead shot Matt Watts about dinnertime today. And by the time the story was brought up here by Babe, it was all wrong."

The boy wished he could get the story faster, but he

waited. He wanted to interrupt and ask Ollie if he heard a dog barking, but Ollie closed the kitchen door, and then it came only very faintly to Aaron.

"Babe was coming along the road early this morning," Ollie continued. "He saw you come out of the hollow and turn up toward Matt Watts's, with Rowdy. When he heard that somebody got shot at Matt Watts's place, arguing over money for a dog, he came shufflin' and sputterin' straight for your house, askin' for you and tellin' the story. Your pa came runnin' past here, for right away he figured it was you who was shot. He was goin' to get the storekeeper to go an' git the body in his pickup truck. This musta been about two hours after dinnertime, middle of the afternoon.

"Who was shot, then? I wasn't," the boy said.

"I just told you, Lon Mead shot Old Matt. The way the storekeeper heard it, and one of the Crowe boys came down to get Mr. Hutton to open the store and call the sheriff. There ain't no phones up around Matt's place. Well, what Mr. Hutton told your pa was that Lon Mead lent Matt two dollars to give to you outside, saying he'd pay Lon as soon as they went to the house. But when they went inside to dinner, after you'd gone, Lon asked Matt for his two dollars and Matt said he'd have to pay later; he didn't have it. An argument started. Matt ordered Lon out of his house. Lon started out, picked up his shotgun that was standin' on the porch loaded, and filled Matt's belly full of buckshot right through the screen door. They was all drunk. At least that's what your pa heard when he walked all the way up there looking for you. He didn't get back here until nearly dark. All the while, we didn't know no better. We still thought it was you that was shot."

"I got to go! Pa'll be terrible mad 'cause he had to walk all that way and didn't find me."

"But let me tell you what else happened. You know the way Tom Ruffner rides over the pastures every Sunday afternoon with the salt bag across his saddle, pourin' some to the flat rocks for the stock? Well, he rode up here and complained about my two lambs, said they were crawlin' under my fence into his field. Said they were there right then.

"I didn't even answer him. I just looked straight up where he was fidgetin' in the saddle and makin' the leather squeak and told him Babe's story. Then I said, 'Mr. Ruffner, you killed that boy. Fer makin' him take back that harmless dog. You killed that boy. And Jake Skinner and the storekeeper has gone to git his body in the storekeeper's pickup truck!' "

"What'd he say?" the boy asked, thinking of his dream and Tom Ruffner being buried standing up like old Mrs. Keck.

"He just sat up there, listenin' to the bit rattle in the horse's mouth. The saddle didn't even squeak. He was froze stiff.

"Then I said, when he'd been settin' quiet for a long time and hadn't even started tappin' the big roan side of the head with the switch, 'Mr. Ruffner, that was a harmless dog. And if he was here right now I could say, 'Rowdy, go git them lambs back.' And he'd herd them back under the fence. I kept him here a month for the boy. And when that dog saw me wavin' my stick and peckin' along the fence after them lambs, he learnt right away. Why, it and that boy could have saved you a lot of trouble gettin' strays out of the bushes when snow falls.'

"Then, after a long time, the saddle squeaked and I thought he was leavin'. But he said in a whisper-like, choked way, 'I've got to sit down,' and he got off his horse and set right here on the pump cement. That was the first time I ever knowed him to be off his horse. You know how he always was sayin' 'By God' this and 'By God' that? 'By God, Ollie Cantrell, if you don't keep them lambs out of my pasture.' Well he didn't say it once. I could feel him changin'; he wasn't the same man that rode up."

Aaron Skinner could not quite think of Thomas Ruffner being changed, but he listened.

"When he'd been still as death for a long time, he said, 'I'd give a thousand dollars if I hadn't done it. Nobody said that dog was used to sheep.' "

"With Old Matt dead and all them dogs shut up in the hogpen, they'll starve." The boy had now sufficiently gotten over the first shock of the story so that his thoughts were for Rowdy. "I dreamed — " and then he stopped short. He was not going to tell his strange dream; no one would believe it, not even the part about Rowdy's escape. "Maybe I can get Rowdy back if Mr. Ruffner knows he's good around sheep."

Ollie Cantrell kept to his own topic. "Then, when he'd been settin' a long while longer and the big roan had wandered over to chomp on the grapevine, he kept saying, 'I'd give a thousand dollars if it had never happened. When do you think they'll be comin' with the boy's body, Ollie?' He'd never called me Ollie before; it had always just been 'Cantrell' or 'By God, Cantrell' or 'Cantrell, by God.' I said they could be along anytime. Jake has been gone two hours or more; but with the sheriff in charge it might take a while."

"I oughta be gittin' home. Pa will skin me sure."

"Your pa'll be so glad you're safe he won't say nothin'. Just one more thing happened before he went away. I could tell the horse was chompin' on the grapevine, 'cause the fence was rattlin'. 'Ollie,' he says, and his head was down in his hands, 'help me to my horse?'

"I did, and he still had his head in his hands. I could tell by his breathin' through his hands. Well, he was limp as a drunk man, missed the stirrup three or four times and me feeling along the flank tryin' to hold it for him.

"And then he rode off without a word. And I heard the horse at a slow walk 'til they were outa hearin'."

"I've got to go. You think he'll let me get Rowdy back if I can?"

"If he don't, I'm as blind as a bat when it comes to seein' change in a man," Ollie said with a quiet snicker as he stood in the kitchen door.

"What I forgot! Did ma send Sara to pick up the milk?"

"Yes, she did. And that little girl was chokin' up with every word. So you hurry on home."

Aaron Skinner stopped and listened several times even

though he was in a great hurry. He was almost sure he heard the clipped end of a bark once.

He put one foot on the stone by the kitchen door, and a bark loud enough to shake the windows came from inside. In one more step the door was open and boy and dog stood facing each other.

Down on his knees Aaron Skinner hugged Rowdy's head close against his heart. It was beating louder than when he had sat upright after the dream behind Ike Eastman's house. Tears rolled down his cheeks. Part of his dream was true. Rowdy had escaped and come home. The corners of the boy's mouth turned up. He took the collar from his pocket and buckled it on the dog. Great tears rolled down his cheeks; the turned-up corners of his mouth caught them.

"I wonder how he got away?" the boy asked when he was able to speak.

"They said he went out through the peak of the roof," Jake Skinner answered. "I walked all the way there to find you. Where'd you go?"

"I went behind Ike Eastman's old house and went to sleep in the sun and didn't wake up 'til late."

"They said at Matt's that Rowdy was shot at. Said Matt and Lon was havin' an argument whether Lon had hit him or not before they got to fightin' over the two dollars."

"Ollie says Mr. Ruffner was awful broke up when everybody thought it was me that was shot. Ollie says he'll let me keep Rowdy, 'cause he told him that Rowdy was good around sheep."

"Well, that might be," Jake Skinner volunteered. "You eat your supper now and go to bed. It's been a mighty tiresome day."

"You scared ten years off our lifetimes," Sophie Skinner said. But there was a softness in her voice which the boy hardly expected, he was so late for supper.

Before the boy said good-night and went to his little room, he pulled Sara and Seth close to him and whispered, "If Mr. Ruffner lets me keep Rowdy, and I'm goin' to ask him right in the mornin' before school, I'll give you each a dollar bill. I promise."

As Aaron Skinner crossed the fields in the dawnlight to be at Thomas Ruffner's big stucco house and back before school-bus time, he hoped Ollie's prediction would come true. He also was possessed with a new feeling about Mr. Ruffner, that Mr. Ruffner had changed and wouldn't be so mean any more.

The boy whistled as he pounced along with Rowdy in the brisk November morn to Mr. Ruffner's back door. There were voices inside the kitchen, so Aaron didn't hesitate to knock. Everybody knew Mr. Ruffner was an early riser; he'd been seen ridin' his land at dawn lots of times. After the boy had knocked several times, he heard a chair scrape on the floor inside. He had his speech right ready. As soon as the door opened, he started, "Mr. Ruffner, Ollie — " but he stopped short.

It was Mr. Dudley, the preacher, who opened the door. Far back in the house someone was moaning.

"I wanted to ask Mr. Ruffner," the boy finally said when Mr. Dudley seemed waiting.

But now he interrupted the boy. "You won't be able to see Mr. Ruffner. He's dead."

The boy walked slowly back across the fields with his dog. He did not whistle as he went.

Thomas Ruffner had hanged himself on a beam in his horse barn with the bridle reins of his big roan stallion, the horse with the nervous mouth.

WILLIAM H. ARMSTRONG received the 1970 Newbery Medal and the 1972 Mark Twain Award for his novel *Sounder*. His other books include *Study is Hard Work, Peoples of the Ancient World, 87 Ways to Help Your Child in School, Through Troubled Waters, Sour Land, Animal Tales, Barefoot in the Grass: The Story of Grandma Moses, Hadassah: Esther, the Orphan Queen,* and *The MacLeod Place*. He is on the faculty of Kent School, in Kent, Connecticut, where he lives on a rocky hill farm dotted with sheep in a house he built with his own hands.